Secret Skeleton

Marsha Sabin Pester

Cover & interior design by
Typewriter Creative Co.

Cover image by Dvid
Interior graphics by Freepik.com

ISBN 979-8-9871053-2-0 (Paperback)
ISBN 979-8-98710-53-3-7 (eBook)

Dedication

For Mom and Dad
Kate and Jerry

And for my siblings
Carolyn
Delbert
Patricia
Catherine

We never did explore the attic, did we?
Hmmm

Prologue

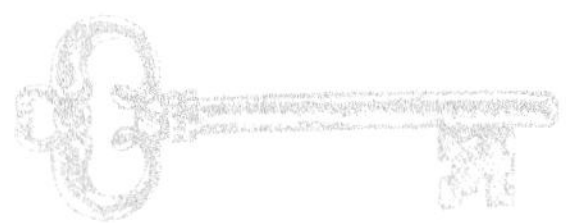

Louis pointed to a trunk, "There's a trunk in that corner. Maybe it has something interesting in it."

The pair walked to the trunk and were about to open it when Louis stepped back, "Look! What's that?" He was standing to the side of the trunk and pointing to something behind it.

Darlene stood directly in front and leaned over, "It just looks like a pile of dirty rags to me."

Louis, who was closer to the object told her, "Look again."

Darlene walked to the side for a better view and gasped, "Is that a skeleton?"

"It sure looks like one. Do you think it's real?"

Chapter 1

April 1, 1965

"Eeoow, Mommy, make Louis stop! He's pulling my hair," yelled seven-year-old Connie. She ran beside her mother, who was in the dining room trying to iron.

Judy Hunt placed the iron on its heel and her hands on her hips, "You kids cut it out! I'm tired of your bickering." It was April first and a blizzard was howling outside. School had been canceled. Twelve-year-old Louis had been tormenting his sister Connie, most of the morning.

"Betty, I could use some help from you!"

This comment was directed at Judy's oldest daughter as she sat reading in an overstuffed chair in the living room. Judy had always liked the name Betty. She had argued, if she named her first born Elizabeth, people would call her Betty anyway. So, she just gave her the name Betty.

"What did you say Mom?"

"I said-get your nose out of that magazine and help me with your brother and sisters!"

"What can I do?"

"Play a game with them. Play...play hide-and-seek."

"Really, Mom? I'm almost sixteen. That's a little old for hide-and-seek. Can't Darlene play with them? She's kinda' childish anyway."

"You brat, I am not," uttered fourteen-year-old Darlene, as she walked into the dining room from the kitchen.

"Girls, please, I need your help." Just then three-year-old Gloria began to cry. "Now you've upset the baby."

"What did we do?" Both girls uttered simultaneously, as they looked at each other.

"Please, I can't take much more. Betty, get the pouting chair. Sit it beside me so you're facing the wall. The rest of you go hide. Connie, take Gloria with you and hide together."

"Oh, Mommy! She always jumps out and says, 'Here I am!' Why can't she hide with Louis or Darlene?"

"Just do as I say. Now go hide." The old farm house had been built before the turn of the century and had many hidey-holes. She was hoping the children would be quiet and it would take Betty a long time to find them.

"Make sure Betty doesn't peek," Darlene said as she and Betty made faces at each other.

Betty continued to look through her teen magazine as the other four children went in different directions.

Judy always ironed in the dining room. It was a bright room with a door leading to a side porch and two large windows all on the north side. The east side had a huge opening into the cheerful living room. An enclosed stairway on the south side of the dining room led to the second floor. The basement door was under these stairs and opened into the dining room. A door on the west side of the dining room led into the kitchen.

Judy watched the children scatter then looked at her oldest and thought, "Almost sixteen! Dear God, You know I love my children. Please give me patience and help me not to get so upset with them."

"Mommy did you hear me?"

"What, Sweetheart?"

"I said, I wish we had a bathtub. It would be so nice to sit and soak in bubbles. Look at this picture." The picture showed a rosy cheeked teen, with her curly blond hair caught up with ribbons, luxuriating in suds up to her neck. She was surrounded by beautiful fixtures and multiple plants.

"Well, if we had a tub there wouldn't be enough water for you to fill it anyway.

Besides, you know someone would be banging on the door, wanting in."

The bathroom upstairs was the only one in the house. It had a small water heater that had to be lit manually. Most of the time, it only got lit on Saturday evenings for quick showers. The rest of the week, water was heated on the kitchen stove for washing at the sink. Cistern water was used for the hot water tank because it was soft. Judy knew that her husband, Lou, had to do something to change all the water to well water during very dry periods. She had never learned how to do it.

"Well, when I get married, I'm going to marry someone rich and adventurous. I want someone different than anyone I've ever known."

"Better stick with someone like

yourself. Being man and woman is different enough.”

“Mommy, have you always been in love with Daddy?”

“No. Growing up, your Aunt Valerie, Dad’s sister, and I were best friends. They lived two blocks down the street from us. Aunt Valerie and I were at each other’s homes all the time. Your dad is four years older than me. He was always coming and going and I just accepted him as part of her family. Then one day, he came in while we were listening to records and looked at me. I thought, ‘Wow, Lou is really cute!’ I was thirteen and he was seventeen. The war was on and he quit school to join the Navy. He was gone for most of the next four years.

“When the war was over, he came home. I was seventeen and he was twenty-one.

He asked me out on a date. Grandpa Seymour said there was no way he would let his seventeen-year-old daughter date a twenty-one-year-old sailor." Judy laughed as she remembered this.

"What did you do, sneak out?"

"Oh no. Your daddy asked Grandpa if I could come to supper at his house with the rest of the family, then go to church on Sunday night. Well, I had never been to a Sunday night church service. I wasn't sure what to expect. Grandpa said it was okay if we rode in the family car with everyone else.

"During the service, after the part with congregational singing, the pastor asked for testimonies. I had no idea what he meant. It was quiet for a few seconds then people started taking turns, standing and telling what God was doing in their lives. Then your dad stood up!

"I couldn't imagine what he was about to say, but I'll never forget what he said. He told about when he enlisted, how a lot of the fellows at school had said he would never stay a Christian and be in the service. Then he quoted Romans 5:20, 'But where sin abounded grace did much more abound.' Before he sat down, he added, 'I want you to know, that verse is true.' Right then I decided he was the man I wanted to marry. We started dating after that and married the day after I graduated from high school. I've never regretted that decision."

Just then Gloria walked into the room. Judy stopped ironing Lou's white shirt and put the iron on its heel, "What are you doing? You're supposed to be hiding."

"I got tired of waiting. Connie wants to

know when you're going to come find her. I can help you, 'cause I know where she's hiding."

"Gloria, don't be telling. You stay here with me and let Betty find Connie by herself."

Betty got up from the pouting chair with a sigh and started towards the living room. In a loud whisper Gloria giggled, "She's behind the couch."

Connie jumped out from behind the couch, wailing, "Mommy, that's not fair! Gloria's always messing up our fun."

"Connie, it's a game. You need to help Gloria learn how to play. There is still Louis and Darlene to find."

"He's under the bed in Betty's room," volunteered Gloria.

"Thanks Gloria," shouted, the dust-bunny-covered Louis, as he crawled out from under the bed.

An angry Betty, with hands on her hips, glared at Louis, "How many times have I told you brats not to go into my bedroom!" Betty's bedroom was directly off the living room. Originally it had been the main entrance vestibule to the house. An armoire now stood in front of the old doorway. A peach tree had sprung up, from a discarded pit, directly in front of the small porch.

"Betty, help me get lunch ready. The rest of you kids go find Darlene."

Darlene had quietly gone into the kitchen, which was a later addition to the old farm house. Off the kitchen was a small room. No one knew its intended use. Everyone in the family called it 'the shed'. It was unheated with a door opening to the outside. This door was boarded shut because the porch had fallen down. Another door opened to stairs leading to the attic over the kitchen. Darlene had softly opened this door and had gone up a couple of steps before closing it. She heard her brother open the door from the kitchen to the shed. She quietly crept up to the attic. Only faint light came through a small round window. Black walnuts on old newspapers covered a large portion of the floor. No one knew how long or why the nuts were up there; neither did they care. No one in the family liked black walnuts. Besides it was too difficult to get the meat out. Mother had told the children, the walnuts had been there when the family moved into the house, fifteen years ago, in 1950.

"She's not in here."

Connie pushed Louis from behind. "See if she went up the stairs."

"Keep your dirty hands off me."

"They're not dirty!"

Both children peeked up the stairs. Connie hugged Louis's arm. "It's dark up there."

"Connie, let go of me! Darlene! Are you up there? Everyone's been found. You can come down if you're up there." Slowly he started up the stairs.

Darlene looked around for some place to hide. There was nothing except the walnuts. Then she cocked her head. What was that? She walked over to a wall just as Louis's head appeared at the opening to the stairs. "I figured this is where you'd be. Come on down. Mom and Betty are fixing lunch. What are you doing?'

Darlene was looking up towards the ceiling. "I think that's a door up there by the ceiling. It looks like it's nailed shut. Go get a flashlight and a hammer."

Just then Betty yelled from the open kitchen door, "You kids get down here. Lunch is ready. You need to wash."

Louis started down the stairs. "Come on, I'm hungry. This'll have to wait until after lunch."

Lunch was peanut butter and grape jelly sandwiches, milk and peaches that Judy had canned last fall. Darlene did not like grape jelly so she had peanut butter on both slices of her bread. "You're going to get fat eating all that peanut butter," warned Betty.

"Well, you're not even going to have the strength Samson had, after Delilah cut off his hair, the way you eat." Betty had one slice of bread with an almost invisible amount of jelly spread on it.

"Girls, please, can't you ever say anything nice to each other? I'm so tired of you two constantly bickering."

"I'm sorry Mom."

"Me too, I just won't talk to Betty anymore. Besides I have something interesting to do after lunch."

"And I'm going to help her," added Louis.

"What are you two up to?" questioned Betty.

Darlene ignored Betty and looked at her mother, "I think there's a door nailed shut in the attic over this kitchen. Louis and I are going to get it open to see what's behind it."

Louis looked at his mom with wide-dark eyes, "Maybe there's a treasure and we'll all be rich!"

"That's just an opening to the old roof. To make this kitchen addition fit onto the original part of the house a dormer window had to be removed. Then the new roof was attached to the old part."

Betty pushed herself away from the table. " Yikes, Mom, do you see what Gloria is doing?" Gloria had smashed her sandwich flat, then proceeded to roll it until it was in a ball. She speared the ball with a fork and was now nibbling around the ball.

Judy smiled at Gloria, "That's exactly what you used to do when you were little Betty."

"Oh, I never would have done such a revolting thing as that!"

"Yes, you did Betty. I know because you taught me to do that," put in Darlene.

Judy looked at Betty with a smile and raised eyebrows, "Before either of you girls do anything, I want you to clean up the kitchen. Connie, when Gloria is finished eating, take her upstairs and wash her hands, then put her down for her nap. I'm going to go lay down myself."

"I helped fix lunch, make Darlene clean up."

"Don't sass me young lady. Do as I say."

Betty glared daggers at Darlene as she started to put the lunch items away.

Chapter 2

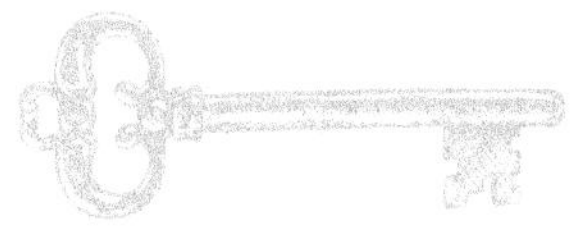

Darlene gave Louis orders as she washed the lunch dishes, "Louis, go out to Dad's workshop and get a hammer. Then find the flashlight. Make sure it works."

Louis put on his coat, boots and hat. Betty stopped him at the back door, "You kids better be careful using Dad's tools. He'll skin you alive if anything is messed up or missing."

"I'll be sure to put the hammer back when we're done." Louis tramped out the door, letting it slam shut behind him.

"Darlene, have you ever known Mom to lie down in the middle of the day?"

"Well, we're in school most days. Weekends, I suppose she doesn't have time. Why? You think she's sick?"

"I don't know. I sure hope not."

When Louis returned and the girls were finished in the kitchen, Betty went to her room to polish her nails. Darlene and Louis returned to the kitchen attic. Darlene turned on the flashlight that glowed very faintly. "Why are the batteries in this always bad? I've never once used this flashlight and had it be bright."

"Turn it off. There's enough light to see for now. We might need it once we get that door open." Louis stood gazing up. "Look at that door. It really doesn't even look like a real door. The bottom part of this wall looks like it's part of the house's original outside wall. That top part looks like large pieces of wood. To me it looks like someone cut a rectangle in the wall above the old wood siding. There aren't any hinges holding the door. I think once we get all the nails removed, the thing is just going to fall out." Louis was almost as tall as Darlene. He had sandy brown hair and his mother's dark eyes. Schooling came very easy to him which annoyed Darlene. She didn't like school and struggled to get C's.

"You'll have to go down to the kitchen and get a chair to stand on. That door is too high to reach from the floor." Without saying a word, Louis faked a salute and trotted down to the kitchen and returned with a chair.

Darlene grabbed the chair and climbed

onto it to have a closer look. "You'd better be careful with that chair. Mom will be really angry at us if you break it."

Large spikes had been driven half way in, on the part of the wall above the original siding, then bent over the door. "I'm surprised we've never noticed this before."

"Really, Darlene, just how many times have you been up here in the last fourteen years?"

"More than you. Come on, let's get this open."

They took turns using the claw end of the hammer to pry up the heads of the nails that were securing the door.

As Louis steadied the chair for Darlene, he asked, "Do you still get spankings?"

"For heaven's sake, no!"

"Well, what do Mom and Dad use for punishment if they don't spank you?"

"Well, last November I had a book report to write. I looked in the library for a short book. I never read books longer than 150 pages. I have so much to do that I don't have time to read longer ones. Anyway, Betty offered. I didn't ask her to do this," Darlene asserted as she held up her hand, like a traffic cop. "She offered to write a book report for me, if I paid her fifty cents. She said she had one due anyway and I could copy hers, just changing it a little. That's what I did. I got an A on my report. Since we are in different grades and have different teachers, she also used the report. She only got a B, which made her really mad. The dummy griped about it to Mom. Mom got mad at both of us. We couldn't go anywhere for a week. That didn't bother Betty much because she's a homebody anyway. But I missed the homecoming game."

"I didn't know you liked football."

"Oh, I don't care about the game. I just like hanging out with my friends."

"Did your teacher ever find out that Betty wrote the report?"

"Y'know, she didn't. Mom never made me tell."

During this conversation the children had changed places. Louis bent back the last nail and got down from the chair. Nothing happened. The two stood looking at the door as if their eyes could make it fall.

Louis pushed the chair to one side and climbed back up. "Stand to the side Darlene. I'll try to put the hammer claw between the boards at the top and get it to open."

The original saw cut was not wide enough to allow the claw between the boards. He gave a terrific smack at the base of the door. Nothing happened. He struck the door several more times. After the fifth blow, the door fell, hitting him and knocking him off the chair. He pushed the door away smiling sheepishly at Darlene.

"You hurt?"

"Naaw. Connie's hit me harder than that."

"What are you children doing? Do you realize Mom and Gloria are trying to nap? She sent me up here to tell you two to BE QUIET!" The brother and sister turned to see Betty's head just above the floor level.

"Well, you certainly aren't being very quiet, Miss Loud Mouth."

"Oh, you're impossible!" Betty turned and disappeared down the steps."

"Let's get this door out of our way and see what was behind it."

The door was surprisingly heavy. The horizontal boards had narrow strips of wood nailed to the back. Once they got it moved, they both stood on the chair and peeked inside. Darlene turned on the flashlight. Facing them was the original roof. They stood looking at it for several seconds. Then they noticed a dark hole where the dormer had been.

"I bet that leads to the attic over the other part of the house. Let's climb in." Louis had already started climbing as he said this. Darlene followed, the flashlight shining a weak beam in front of her. Louis dropped to the floor of the old attic and helped Darlene down off the roof. He was surprised that she didn't complain about his help. There was a very dirty window on the other side of the attic. Both siblings stood looking about the dim area. Without being asked, Louis removed his handkerchief from his pocket, walked to the window and began wiping off years of grime.

Whenever he went anywhere his dad usually asked him if he had a handkerchief. Louis once asked his dad why men always carried handkerchiefs. His father had replied, "To give to a lady when she starts to cry." Louis didn't understand this answer. His dad had told him that one day he would.

"Look at this place, after all that work of getting the door open, and it's only full of old furniture and a rolled-up rug," Darlene uttered disappointedly.

Louis pointed to a trunk, "There's a trunk in that corner. Maybe it has something interesting in it."

The pair walked to the trunk and were about to open it when Louis stepped back, "Look! What's that?" He was standing to the side of the trunk and pointing to something behind it.

Darlene stood directly in front and leaned over, "It just looks like a pile of dirty rags to me."

Louis, who was closer to the object told her, "Look again."

Darlene walked to the side for a better view and gasped, "Is that a skeleton?"

"It sure looks like one. Do you think it's real?"

"Probably not, it looks like it's wearing

some kind of fancy dress, or what's left of it. Maybe it was a wedding dress. I bet it's from some long-ago Halloween party. Whoever lived in this house before us put it up here and forgot about it."

"I think we'd better not touch it. We should tell Mom."

"Well, okay. I still don't think it's real."

Chapter 3

Judy was sitting in the living room with her feet resting on a stool. She and Betty were watching **Days of Our Lives**. Darlene and Louis raced into the room. "Mom, you'll never guess what we found in the attic," blurted out Louis before Darlene had a chance to say anything.

"I hope it's worth you waking me up with all that loud racket you two made."

"We're sorry Mom. Anyway, we found a skeleton! A real live skeleton!"

"Shhhhhh! I can't hear my story,"

complained Betty. "And how can a skeleton be alive?"

Louis looked at Betty with a smirk, "Okay, it's not alive. But Mom, there's a skeleton in the attic!"

"Yes, and today is April 1st. If you think you two children are going to April fool me, you've got another think coming Buster!"

"Mommy, there is a skeleton up there. Please come and look," Darlene pleaded.

"I'm not about to get out of this chair and climb a bunch of stairs. Then crawl along the roof."

Just then they heard a noise outdoors. Louis ran to the window and sighed, "It's the snow plow. I guess we'll have school tomorrow."

"Who cares?" Darlene turned and ran

up the stairs to her bedroom. She came back carrying a Polaroid® Instant camera. It had been a Christmas gift from her grandparents. "Come on Louis, I'll take a picture to show Mom." The two started back to the attic.

Judy called after them, "Don't take more than one picture. That film costs fifty cents a shot."

Louis ran ahead, racing up the stairs. He stood beside the trunk pointing to the skeleton.

 "Louis, get out of the way. I only want the skeleton." Louis gave Darlene a sour look as he moved away. Darlene very carefully aimed the camera and snapped a picture. The exposed picture came sliding out of the camera. "Quick, we have to get downstairs. I need to put the jell on it.

That fixes the picture so the image doesn't disappear."

Judy could see what looked like a skeleton sticking out from behind the trunk. "It's a skeleton alright. The question is, 'Is it real?'" Wide eyed, the children looked at each other. "I guess we should leave everything as it is. I'll call the sheriff, and let him decide what to do." Judy really couldn't care less. She had other things on her mind.

Sighing with a hint of exhaustion, Judy got up and called the sheriff's office. The only phone in the house was located in the dining room. This always annoyed Betty, something fierce. She didn't like others being able to hear her conversations.

The children stood around their mother listening to the one-sided conversation. The phone rang a long time before being answered. "Hi Thelma, this is Judy Hunt." Thelma had worked at the sheriff's office since graduating from high school seven years ago. Her father had been the grade school principal for over twenty years. Everyone knew the family. "I'm fine. No, there's nothing wrong. Well, in a way there is. I'm calling to let the sheriff know my children found a skeleton in our attic."

After a long pause Judy continued, "Thelma, I know most families have skeletons in their closets. Ours is in the attic. No, I don't know if it's real. It's probably a left-over Halloween decoration or something. Before we move it, I'd like someone to check it out."

Judy listened, then said, "The plow just came by. The road is open, but not our driveway. Whoever comes will have to park out on the road and walk in."

The driveway was about one hundred feet long. No one ever plowed it. Louis Hunt Senior was a truck driver who was allowed to drive his truck home. Once he got home, he would drive up and down over the snow to pack it down.

"That's okay. This isn't an emergency. The skeleton has been up there at least fifteen years. Another day or so won't matter. I'll see that the children stay out. Thank you. You too, goodbye."

"What did she say?"

"Is the sheriff coming?"

"Please, children. The sheriff and his deputies are very busy. There are a lot of accidents because of the weather. Thelma said it might be tomorrow before anyone has time to come here." Judy walked to the kitchen and picked up a chair setting it down in front of the shed door. "Don't any of you move this chair. It's to stay right here."

"That's Daddy's chair. How's he going to eat sitting way over there?" questioned Connie.

"Well, it just better be sitting there when Daddy comes home tonight. Now go find something to occupy yourselves with. And I don't mean teasing or fighting."

Betty came flying into the kitchen as her mother was preparing supper. "Mom, Sean O'Toole is walking up the drive!" Betty stood at a kitchen window and watched Sean make his way towards the house. "Oh! Isn't he the most handsome man you've ever seen!"

Deputy Sean had worked for the county for four years after being discharged from the Army. Judy knew Sean had been a "whoops" baby. He was ten years younger than his closest sibling.

"Betty, you mind your manners! You're not even sixteen. Sean is twenty-five."

"Mom, just look at him!" Sean had black curly hair and deep blue eyes. There was a dimple in each of his rosy cheeks. Everyone spoke well of him, saying he had the personality of a true Irishman.

Betty opened the kitchen door before Sean had a chance to knock. No one ever came to the front door. Most people didn't even realize there was a front door. "Hello Betty. How are you today? I hear you're scaring up ghosts."

"Not me. It's my little sister and brother. Come on in."

"Hello Mrs. Hunt."

"Good afternoon, Sean. I'm sorry you had to walk from the road."

"Oh, I don't mind at all. It actually felt kind of good after riding around all day. So, tell me about your ghost."

"I hope it's not a ghost. This kitchen was added on to the house years ago. There is an attic over it that is connected to the older part of the house. The children were playing hide-and-seek and noticed a door that had been nailed shut up there. They worked it open and climbed into a hole. The hole is a result of a dormer window being removed. I guess that way the builders were able to attach the new roof onto the old house. The children found what appears to be a skeleton in the original attic."

"You didn't know about the door before?"

"I knew a way to get to the old part was there. But, that's all. I was only up there once when we first moved here."

"Did you go up today to look at the skeleton?"

"No, I didn't. Darlene took this picture with her Polaroid®. It's a skeleton. I don't know if it's real or just a fake. Perhaps it's left over from a Halloween decoration."

Sean looked at the picture, "Well, it does look real. Show me where it is."

Betty started to move the chair from in front of the door. "I will!"

"No, you will not!" voiced her mother. "Louis, show Deputy O'Toole up to the attic."

Louis moved the chair and opened the door leading into the shed area. Sean followed and as he passed Betty, he smiled and gave Betty a wink. Betty thought she might faint.

Sean stopped and looked around the shed area. There was not much to see. "Is this room used?"

"Not really. We mostly store junk in here." Strewn around the room were empty boxes, an old table and other odd pieces. Sean looked these over before turning his attention to the door leading to the small attic.

"Now, am I right in thinking this is not the door that was nailed shut?"

"Yes sir, this door leads to the attic over the kitchen. There's another door once you get up there." Louis opened the door and started up the stairs.

"Louis, let me go first, please." Louis

stepped aside and Sean started up the stairs. He pulled his flashlight from his service belt and turned it on. The walnuts were the first things he saw. "Are you saving these for some reason?"

"No, they've been here since as long as I can remember."

Sean bent down on one knee and lifted the edge of one of the newspapers under the walnuts. "This newspaper is from 1935! Thirty years! That's almost unbelievable." He stood up and looked at the door that had been removed which was now leaning against the wall.

"That's the door me and Darlene took off. You have to stand on the chair and crawl up the old roof to get to the other attic."

Sean stepped onto the chair and shined his light into the darkness then up to the hole.

Louis stood watching him. Sean turned to Louis before climbing onto the old roof, "Thanks Louis. I may be up here awhile. You can go back down."

Disappointed, Louis turned to leave as Sean climbed onto the roof then through the hole into the old attic.

Once by himself Sean walked over to the trunk. He moved his flashlight to see behind it. There lay the skeleton. It was surrounded by several dirty stained rags. An old rope was around the neck bones. It looked very real. Remnants of a lace dress were still distinguishable around the bones. He looked about the attic a bit longer and saw what he believed to be another access. This one was in the floor. It was also nailed shut. He examined the skeleton and the surrounding area carefully before returning to the kitchen. All five children were standing, staring at him.

"I'm no expert, but it does appear to be a real skeleton. I'll have to seal this door for now. The coroner will come out and verify if it's real. I have some door seals in the car; I'll be right back."

Louis's eyes were the size of saucers, "Jiminy Cricket! He's putting crime seals on the door. Boy, wait 'til the guys at school hear about this."

Judy sighed and thought, "Just wait until Lou gets home and sees the door sealed shut."

Louis Senior worked for one of the transportation contractors for the local automobile plant. His boss was very fond of him. He allowed Lou to drive his truck home every night. Lou mainly worked moving trailers from one factory building to another. Sometimes he'd make short hauls to near-by cities such as Detroit or Lansing. This would occur during the early spring thaw when there were weight restrictions on the highways. On days like today he was often late getting home because he stopped to help stranded drivers who didn't have enough sense to slow down in bad weather and ended up in ditches. Judy didn't expect him until late.

Chapter 4

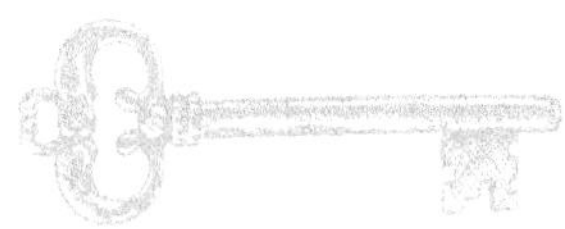

It was after seven when Lou finally drove up the long lane leading to the house. He drove back and forth several times before coming in. Judy had kept his supper warm in the oven. She set it on the table as he opened the kitchen door. Before she said a word their five children surrounded him all talking at once about the day's adventure.

"Hold on there, I can't understand a word that's being said. What's all this about the shed door being sealed?"

"Children, leave your father alone. Sit down

and you can have some cookies as Daddy eats. Mind you, no more than two apiece."

Lou was more hungry than curious. After five children, not much surprised him anymore. He began to eat as the children took their places around the table. Mom poured each a small glass of milk and placed a cookie plate in the middle of the table. Louis sat on a folding chair because his chair had been left in the attic.

While Lou and the children were quietly eating, Judy filled him in on the day's adventure. "Lou, Darlene and Louis discovered the door in the small attic over the kitchen that was nailed shut. They managed to pull out the nails. After removing the door, they climbed onto the roof and through the dormer hole into the main attic and found a skeleton."

"What! Was it just a Halloween decoration?"

"We don't know. I called the sheriff's department. Sean O'Toole came out and had a look around. He thinks it's real. That's why the seal is on the door."

Louis interrupted his mother, "And that's why I have to sit on this folding chair. My chair is still up in the attic."

"The coroner is coming out tomorrow to have a look. We aren't to go up to the attic until the coroner comes," continued Judy.

"The skeleton is wearing a wedding dress," put in Darlene. "And look Daddy. Here's a picture I took."

"Well, I'll be. Coming home is always special, but even this surprises me."

The children had finished their snacks. Judy stood up and began collecting the dirty dishes, "Louis, Connie, Gloria, it's your bed time. Go on up, I'll be there in a couple of minutes to tuck you in."

Connie and Gloria shared a bedroom. Louis had a tiny room which had an outside door with a stairway leading down the backside of the house. Lou had taken out a window and put in the door and stairway. He wanted an emergency way out of the upstairs in case of fire or other danger.

Gloria started to pout, "I'm so tired Mommy, can't you carry me?"

Lou jumped up. "Let me Sweetheart. Your mommy's had a busy day. Kiss Mommy good night." He picked Gloria up, "Come on you two, I'll race you!" Lou took off at a fast pace as Gloria squealed with delight. The other two children raced closely behind.

Judy watched them go and thought. "He's really a good father. Works so hard all day, comes home tired, yet is willing to help with the kids. I hope he doesn't mind another."

Lou returned as Betty and Darlene were leaving the table to go to their bedrooms. "Goodnight Mom. Goodnight Dad," each echoed as they left the room.

Judy, astonished, looked at her daughters, "Well, what prompts you two to head for bed so early?"

"I have some homework to do."

"Darlene, you've been home all day and haven't done your homework? You're just starting it at almost eight o'clock?"

"I know Mom, I really don't like school."

"That doesn't mean you don't have to do your homework. Young lady if you bring home a bad report card, you're going to be in a lot of trouble."

"Yes Mom."

Judy sighed as the girls left the room. "I hope she manages to graduate. What's going to become of her?"

"Probably the same thing that became of her mother, married with a house full of kids. Come here to Papa."

Judy moved to her husband's lap and laid her head on his shoulder. "Speaking of children, what would you say to another?"

"Another what?"

"Baby, you silly."

"Are you……?"

"Yes, I'm pretty sure. I have an appointment with Dr. Tucker next week."

Lou started to laugh with gusto, "Well, it sure has been fun."

"What's so fun Daddy? What's been fun?"

"Hey, young man I thought I just took
you to bed!"

Louis stood in the doorway holding
a kitten, "This cat came in through a
broken window pane. When I caught it, it
scratched me." He raised his left arm to
reveal a small red scratch.

Judy got up from her husband's lap, "Come
over here to the sink so I can wash your
arm. I didn't know there was a broken pane
in your room. How did it happen?"

"Well, I was just trying to get a head start
on baseball and I sort of broke it when I
was practicing my swing this afternoon."

Lou looked at his son for several seconds.
"We need the hammer, some nails
and a board."

Louis looked very downcast, "I think the hammer is still up in the attic. When we found the skeleton, I forgot all about the hammer and didn't put it away. Now we can't go up there to get it." He raised his head and looked at his dad. "I'm sorry Daddy." As he was apologizing, Judy applied Mercurochrome to his arm and then an adhesive bandage. "Ouch Mommy, that hurts."

"Too bad."

"I've got a hammer in my truck. I'll get the nails and a board while I'm out there. You know the cost of the new pane will come out of your allowance, don't you?" Louis nodded. Lou put on his coat and gloves, then held out his hand, "Give me the cat." He walked out to the garage gingerly carrying the cat. He found a box and punched a couple of holes in it. Before placing the cat in the box, he picked up a rag and covered the bottom. He tied string around the box so the cat couldn't get out. Next, he walked to his truck and none too gently tossed the box on the seat and got a hammer out of his tool box. He returned to the garage to gather the other items he would need to temporarily block the broken window.

Louis stuck his head between cupped hands against a kitchen window to watch outside, "Do you think Daddy is real mad at me?"

"He's disappointed in you for doing something you know you shouldn't have. He's also tired and now has to close up your window before he can rest."

Lou returned to the house. He and Louis started up the stairs. "Daddy why were you laughing so hard, what's been fun?"

"Being married to your mom is fun."

"It is? How come?"

"You'll understand when you're older.
Believe me, you'll understand."

While Lou and Louis covered the broken
window, Judy heated water on the stove.
She often gave Lou a "sink" bath on nights
when he had worked late. Lou returned
to the kitchen, sat down and removed
his shirt. Judy took the shirt and tossed
it in a clothes basket, "What did you do
with the cat?"

"It's in a box in my truck. I'll take it with me
tomorrow and drop it off at the vet. I just
hope it doesn't have rabies."

"When you put Louis to bed, did he say
anything to you about getting bit? Did you
see any other scratches on him?" Judy

said this as she lovingly washed Lou's face, neck, arms, and torso.

"No, he didn't. And he didn't have any more scratches, that I noticed. You should probably take a closer look at him tomorrow."

Chapter 5

Sean sat half-dozing, half-watching **The Dean Martin Show** on television. He was tired. About half way through the program, he decided to head for bed. Sean lived on the second floor of an old house that had been converted to apartments. He had two rooms. One was a combination living room and the other was his bedroom. Between the two was a very small bathroom. As he climbed into bed, he heard the wind picking up. He hoped the roads didn't get covered again.

Throughout the night, the wind continued

to blow. It didn't snow again, however, the snow that had fallen earlier began to cover the roads once more.

 Three men hid in the woods, next to Smitty's Beer Garden. Six or eight cars, mostly "clunkers" were parked in the poorly lit lot. These cars were "shop cars" used mainly for driving to and from work at the auto plant.

One car in Smitty's parking lot stood out among the clunkers, a brand-new 1965, Buick Riviera. The Buick belonged to a man named Steve. On payday he carried thousands of dollars in a grocery bag. For a fee, Steve would cash checks for workers, who did not, or would not, use a bank. Some needed immediate money to pay off gambling debts; others wanted cash to stop off at bars on their way home from work. A few didn't want their wives to know how much money they made. Today was payday at the factories.

One thief whispered to Doug, the leader, "Are you sure this is the bar the man goes to?"

"Yes, I've worked with Steve for over a year. He stops here every night before going in to third shift. That new green Riviera next to that '49 black Chevy coupe is his." Pointing, Doug continued, "Ted, you get behind the Chevy. Make sure you stay down so he can't see you when he comes out. When I step out, you go to the passenger side and cover me. Len, get the car. Pull close behind the Buick and when you see Ted and me move towards the car, be ready to get out of here fast." The two men turned to their assigned tasks as Doug had ordered.

Steve came out the door carrying a large

grocery bag, followed by another man. They didn't see Doug as he walked quickly towards the Riviera. Their attention was focused on the approaching auto as Len pulled behind the Riviera, blocking it in.

Steve stopped and yelled at Len, "Hey, what are you doing? Get that car outa' here."

From behind Steve, Doug shouted, "Hands in the air. Don't move and no one gets hurt."

Steve turned, "Why you dirty dog!" Steve bellowed as he pulled a gun and shot Doug. Doug couldn't believe what had happened. He thought this was going to be so easy.

 At that same moment Ted came running out from beside the black Chevrolet and shot at Steve's friend who had been standing by the passenger door terrified. The gravel drive received his wounded body. Ted continued running to the get-away car. "Come on Len, let's get out of here." Len didn't need any more encouragement. He backed out, did a swift turnabout and sped down the blacktop road.

Two sheriff's deputies were on duty that night. A description of the car, a 1958, white over blue Oldsmobile Cutlass, was broadcast to the patrol cars almost immediately. Twenty-three-year-old Donald Torbee, a recent hire, was on his fourth night of patrol. He started down the blacktop towards Smitty's when the offender's car sped passed him, going in the opposite direction. He did a U-turn, activated his lights and siren and raced after the suspects.

Len lost control of the Cutlass as he rounded a notoriously sharp curve with a slight rise on the Drayton blacktop. The blowing snow had caused the road to ice over. The car spun around stopping crossways in the road. Deputy Torbee negotiated the curve before colliding broadside with the Oldsmobile. The passenger side of the Cutlass took the full impact of the collision, killing Ted instantly. Torbee was critically injured, only Len managed to limp away.

Chapter 6

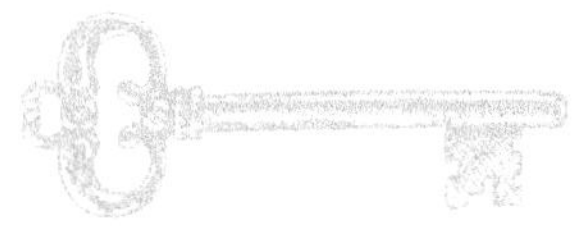

"Darlene! Wake up. You have to get up!"

Darlene rose up on one elbow and looked
at her bedside clock. "Mom, it's only a
quarter to six. Why do I have to get up
so early?"

"The wind blew snow across the back
roads last night. School is open. The buses
are only going on the main highways.
Dad is going to drop you children off at
Grandpa's and Grandma's house in town
on his way to work. Grandma will cook
breakfast for you. Your dad will be leaving
in twenty minutes, so unless you want to

walk the half mile to the highway and wait for the bus, you'd better get up."

"Please, Mom, let me stay home. I'm tired."

"I know you are and I know why. You were up until very late doing homework. Let that be a lesson to you young lady. Now get up! You're going to school."

Judy passed the only bathroom on her way to wake up Louis. She could hear Betty singing along with some rock and roll music. "Hurry up in there Betty. Daddy is leaving in just a few minutes and Darlene and Louis still need to get in there."

"Five minutes, Mom."

"NO, two minutes."

Louis held the box containing the kitten on his lap as Lou drove the children to his parents' home. Judy had let Connie sleep.

She had been up with Connie twice during the night. Connie was having nightmares about the skeleton. She was finally sleeping peacefully and Judy decided she would be too tired in school all day if she had to get up so early.

"Why do I have to leave the kitten in the box, why can't I hold it?"

"Because I don't want it to scratch or bite anyone. It's not a tame animal."

"What are you going to do with it?"

Darlene answered her brother, "It has to be tested for rabies. If it has rabies, you'll have to have shots in your stomach for weeks!"

"Is that true, Daddy?" Louis looked at his dad with a worried frown on his face.

"Darlene, quit scaring your brother."

"Well, it's true. I'm not lying."

Without answering, Lou responded, "Here we are at your grandparents'. Now behave and don't talk about the cat. It will only worry Grandma."

Grandma Hunt was a short, round lady with tightly permed gray hair and beautiful hazel eyes. She wouldn't tell her grandchildren how old she was. She would only say, "I'm as old as my little finger and a little older than my teeth." In truth, she had turned sixty-three on New Year's Day. Her roundness was evidence to the fact that she loved to cook. This morning she stood over the stove making pancakes. A platter of bacon was being kept warm in the oven.

Lou went over to his mom and while giving her a kiss on the cheek asked, "Morning Mom. Where's Dad?"

"He'll be down in a couple of minutes. Sit down. Breakfast is ready."

Lou hadn't planned on staying to eat, but when he saw the pancakes and bacon and real Michigan maple syrup, he changed his mind. Grandpa Hunt entered the kitchen carrying the morning paper.

Louis ran to Walter Hunt, "Grandpa, guess what Darlene and I found in the attic!"

"A ghost!"

"Well, almost. We found a skeleton and Deputy Sean O'Toole came to look at it."

Grandpa looked at his son expecting an explanation.

"That's about all I know too, Dad. There's a skeleton up there. Judy said it looked like it had been dressed in a wedding gown. The coroner is coming to decide if it's real. Did you bring your picture of the skeleton with you, Darlene?"

Darlene joined the conversation, "Yes, I did. Look Grandpa. I'm taking it to school with me to show the kids. The whole attic is sealed off. We can't go up there now."

"I don't see what difference it makes. It's just a bag of bones!" exclaimed Betty as she took one pancake eating it plain with no butter or syrup.

"Just a bag of bones! Betty, at one time, that was a living breathing woman. She had a family. Maybe she was even married and had children. Someone must have loved her and wondered what happened to her."

"I guess you're right. It's just hard for me to imagine that."

Lou looked at his second daughter. Sometimes she truly surprised him. Like now, she seemed to care and empathize for a person she knew nothing about. "I've got to get going or I'll be late for work. Kids, Mom will call the school this afternoon to ask if the buses will run their regular routes. If they don't, come here after school and I'll pick you up on my way home." The children nodded and waved good-bye.

Lou was already running late when he left his folks. It dawned on him that the county pound wouldn't be open yet. He would have to keep the cat with him until his lunch break. Several times during the morning he had to explain to other men why he had a cat in a box on the seat of his truck.

After taking the children to school, Grandpa Hunt drove to the only restaurant in town, **Aunt Patti's Kitchen**. It was the custom of several of the older men in town to gather there of a morning. Any given day there could be two to six or seven men seen sitting in a large booth at the rear of the restaurant. This morning Walter Hunt saw only one man sitting in the customary booth. It was Henry Gullington, a retired Army Warrant Officer. "Gully", as he was nick-named, was a short, well-muscled man with thick white hair and piercing deep blue eyes. He had seen action in both World Wars I and II in the Field Artillery.

He never talked about his exploits during those times of conflict or the medals he had earned. Walter Hunt knew his friend had been in the final battle of World War I. It was known as the Meuse-Argonne battle. He had been assigned to the Second Army. Gully had been awarded the Citation Star for "Gallantry in Action". He had dislodged a shell that had not detonated from an artillery gun when the firing pin struck the fuse. This was known as a "hang fire."

Gully was also with the 111th Field Artillery Battalion at Omaha Beach in 1944, at the D-Day Invasion. All but one gun was lost in the attempt to get them ashore. The battalion fought side by side with the infantry on the beach. Gully was wounded in the battle and awarded a Purple Heart.

 Retiring from the Army, in 1947, he worked as a contract worker with the government for another ten years. Then he and his wife Beverly moved to Leichester. This had been Beverly's childhood home.

Walter slid comfortably into the booth. The waitress brought him a cup of coffee. "Want anything else this morning Walt?"

"Bring me a cake doughnut Sheila." Sheila left to get his doughnut. "Morning Gully."

Gully looked at his friend and asked,

"Did you hear the news on the radio this morning?"

"No, my son brought the grandkids over to wait for school to start. Their road is still closed from the storm yesterday. What news?"

"There was an attempted robbery at Smitty's Beer Garden last night. One robber was shot and killed. Another man wounded. Another of the robbers died when a sheriff's car slammed into the get-away car on the Drayton Blacktop at that bad curve. The deputy was also badly injured."

"Wow, I can't remember when the last time something like that happened around here."

"The radio announcer said it was in 1952 when some bank was held up."

"Yeah, that's right. I remember. A teller was killed. The two robbers were caught by Sheriff Dave Byrne who was at that time a deputy. Some folks say that is how Byrne got to be sheriff. The next election he ran for sheriff and won. I can't say anything bad about him, he's a good man.

"The week the robbers were tried there were State Police up in the cupola of the court house with shot guns. People were real angry at the killers. The teller, Josh Parker was well liked. He was married and had a house full of kids."

Just then Roger Kennedy entered the café and sat down with the two men. "Mornin' fellas. Have you heard the news about the robbery?"

"Yeah, Gully just told me about it. Did the radio say who the robbers were or who got killed?"

"No, but I know!"

Walt looked at his friend skeptically, "And just how do you know?"

"Because, one of them is my neighbor, Doug Lemon. The word is, he was the leader."

"No kidding. Who were the others?"

"Well, according to my wife's sister's husband's cousin, Ted Smith was the other robber killed."

"How does this cousin know that?" Asked Gully, doubtfully.

"He works at the Dessison County Hospital and was there when the two bodies were brought in. He overheard the sheriff talking to the coroner."

"I've always felt sorry for Ted."

"Why's that, Walt?"

"Ted was a replacement baby. He had a brother that was hit by a car when he was about six. His mother decided to "replace" him and had Ted. She was so protective of him. She was determined nothing was going to happen to this son. As a child he was not allowed out of the backyard. Ted's mother drove him to school every day and picked him up after school for twelve years. Consequently, he had very few friends. Now with his mother dead, Ted was adrift without her."

"I also found out that the third robber who got away is Len Rheimes", acknowledged Roger smugly.

"Really? Now that's a surprise." This was volunteered by Gully.

"How do you know Len?" Asked Roger, a bit deflated.

"He's talked to me a couple of times about being in the Army. He always says…"

Roger, Walt, Sheila and two other customers, who had been listening to this conversation said in unison, "I should have stayed in the Army!" Everyone in the café laughed.

Sheila came over to the booth with a cup of coffee for Roger. "Oh, Sheila put that in a paper cup. I can't stay. I've got to get to work."

After Roger left, Walt and Gully sat quietly drinking coffee and eating doughnuts. Walt spoke up, "Say I didn't tell you about my news."

"What would that be?"

"My grandkids were playing hide-and-seek yesterday and found a skeleton in their attic."

"Skeleton! Is it real?"

"No one knows yet. The coroner is going out to the house today to have a look. My granddaughter said it was dressed in what looked to have been a fancy dress like maybe a wedding dress and she even has a Polaroid® picture".

"Is that a fact? How long has it been up in the attic? Hasn't anyone ever gone up there?"

"Evidently not. My son and his family have lived in the house since about 1950. They rent it from my brother Steve."

"Is he the recluse who lives on Elm Street?"

"Yeah, that's him. Steve and his family

used to live in the farmhouse. He and his son moved into town after my sister-in-law and niece died just months apart."

"If the skeleton is real, it must have been up there long before your son moved in. Otherwise, he surely would have smelled it. If it is real, this could prove interesting. Do you know of anybody who went missing a long time ago?"

"I can't say that I do. My wife now, her memory is something else. She can probably remember what she ate for breakfast on Christmas, 1940! She's the one to ask."

"Bev's the same. She hadn't lived here from the time we married in '27 until we moved back in '57; but she can remember every day when she did live here. She's always telling me about when one person got married or when someone else broke his arm, things like that."

"You know, with the attempted robbery and shoot-out that happened last night, I'll bet the sheriff's department won't have much time to put toward finding out about this skeleton. Say, why don't you and Bev come over to our house for lunch? Like you say, this could be really interesting. We can be special investigators. The sheriff is already a man short because Earl Swartz quit to work for the Detroit police. Now he's two men short with Torbee in the hospital. The four of us can sit around and come up with possible women who went missing and were never found."

"Are you sure Joan won't mind our coming without asking her first?"

"Naaw, she'll be tickled pink with trying

to solve the mystery. Why! Her favorite movies are mysteries."

Chapter 7

Just after nine a.m. the snow plow passed the Hunt house pushing snow into the opening of the driveway. It was followed a few minutes later by a sheriff's car. Judy was upstairs in her two middle girls' bedroom and watched as the driver gunned the car to get through the snow. Then the driver carefully followed the tracks Lou's truck had made. She went down stairs in time to open the kitchen door after the second knock. "Good morning Sean, I've been expecting you. Come on in."

Sean was followed by Theo Larkin, who

owned the local meat locker. He was also the county coroner and a second cousin of Judy's. "Good morning, Judy." Theo had grown up in Dessison, an unincorporated area in the northern part of the county. He was a tall, thin man of forty-two. He tried unsuccessfully to comb long side hair over his balding head. Like Judy, he knew most everyone in the area. "Sean tells me you have a skeleton in your closet!" He gave a disagreeable laugh.

There was something about Theo's demeanor that had always bothered Judy. She could not quite put her finger on what it was. Thinking, she was done with 'skeleton in the closet jokes', she put a false smile on her face, "It's not really in the closet, it's in our attic."

"Yes, I know. I was just making a little

joke." An uncomfortable silence followed Theo's remark.

Sean walked to the shed door and removed the seal. "Well, Mr. Larkin, the bones are this way." He opened the door and entered the room followed by the coroner.

Judy watched them as Sean opened the second door going to the stairs. She stood listening to the sound of their steps as they went up to the attic directly over the kitchen. They then crossed to the opening leading to the attic over the old part of the house.

"Mommy, what are you looking at?" Connie stood next to Judy. Judy hadn't heard Connie enter the kitchen.

"Deputy O'Toole and another man are here to look at the skeleton."

"Can I go up and see it?"

"No Connie. It's an investigation. Only special people are allowed up there right now."

"That's not fair."

"Not all things in life are fair. Go see what Gloria is doing. She's been quiet too long."

Judy heard the two men come down the stairs about a half hour later. Pompously and officiously, Theo stated, "Judy, as you probably may not know, we don't have a morgue in this county. The Gordon Funeral Home functions as the county morgue in cases like this. Someone from there will be by later to remove the remains."

Judy thought, "That's it. That's what bothers me about him. He acts so vain." Out loud she asked, "What time do you think they might be here? Now that the road is open, I have some errands to run before the children get home from school."

"I can't say. Can't you wait until they come, before you do your errands? You have a houseful of kids. Aren't the older ones big enough to look after the younger ones if you wait and go later?"

"You didn't answer my question."

Sean gave Theo a side-long glance before saying to Judy, "Mrs. Hunt, I'll tell Mr. Gordon to call first."

"Thanks Sean."

The men had only been gone a little more than an hour when Mr. Gordon from the funeral home called. He asked, "Would it be convenient to come tomorrow morning about eight? The funeral home is very busy just now." Judy said that would be fine.

A second call came later in the day from the local veterinary clinic. It also acted as the county animal control office. The caller was Renee Smith, a longtime receptionist at the office. She was a close friend of Judy's mother-in-law, Joan. Renee and Joan had met in the hospital when Joan was having her fourth child, and Renee was giving birth to her first. They had become good friends. "Dr. Dan said the cat doesn't appear to be sick. Just the same, it has to be quarantined for ten days to be sure it doesn't have rabies. Is the cat yours? Will you be paying for the boarding?"

Judy hesitated and asked what the cost would be for boarding the cat. However, she didn't see any choice but to pay. They needed to know for Louis's sake. Rene understanding Judy's hesitation suggested, "The cat can be put-down and the head sent to the state lab for testing. Would you rather do that?"

 Judy was uncomfortable having the cat killed; however, stray animals were a constant problem. It was not unusual for town people to drop off unwanted pets in the country. The receptionist understood Judy's dilemma, "Judy, I know it's difficult to have an animal killed. However, there will be no charge from the state for the testing. That way there won't be any boarding fee either."

"Yes, that does make a difference. Please send it in for testing. You will let me know?"

"Yes, I will. One more thing, Lou said the kitten scratched your son."

"Yes, it did. I cleaned it with soap and water before putting Mercurochrome and a bandage on it. I looked at it again this morning. It doesn't look bad."

"Good. I'll make arrangements for the state examination and let you know as soon as the results come back."

"Thank you so much. I really appreciate your help."

Judy felt terrible after this conversation. She was also upset with Louis for breaking the window. At first, she was going to tell him what was going to happen to the kitten, then decided not to. She offered up a prayer that the test would be negative.

Later that day Judy received a call from the veterinarian. "Good afternoon, Judy, this is Dr. Dan. Rene said the cat scratched Louis. I think you should call your physician and tell him. He may write a prescription for an antibiotic ointment. Mercurochrome isn't used much anymore."

"What are you concerned about? Was the kitten infectious?"

"No nothing like that. A person can contract a disease known as 'cat scratch fever' which can result in a serious illness. Check with your doctor and keep an eye on the scratch. If Louis runs a fever or shows any unusual symptoms, be sure to let your doctor know."

"Thank you so very much. We surely will, and we appreciate your help." As Judy hung up the telephone, she offered up another prayer.

Three days later Renee Smith called from the animal hospital with the results of the rabies test. It was negative. Judy again thanked the Lord.

Chapter 8

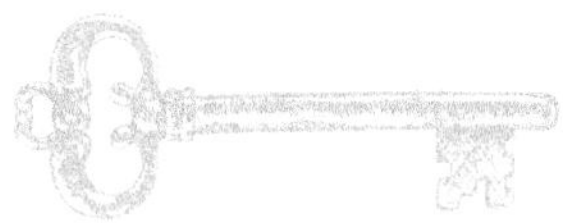

After lunch, four white-haired people sat around the senior Hunt's dining room table talking and drinking coffee. Walt and Joan Hunt had lived in this house for the forty-five years of their marriage. As children were born to the couple, three girls and one boy, rooms had been added on to the original four-room, white clapboard, cape cod house.

The cookies Joan made that morning were almost all gone. She had planned to give them to the grandchildren if they came over after school. Looking at the few remaining cookies Joan wondered if she would have time to bake more.

Bev Gullington interrupted her thoughts, "This is really exciting. What do you think is the best way to go about finding out who the person was?"

Walter nodded to Joan, "Joan, grab the pen and tablet on the buffet. First, let's think about the house. When was it built and who has lived there?"

Bev spoke up with her hand out, "Joan why don't you give me the pen and tablet? You've been busy feeding us and I enjoy being a secretary. Now, the first people I remember living there were the Campbells. They built the house," Bev started telling what she knew. "We lived on the farm about a half mile down and across the road, south of the Campbell farm. It's the house the Reeds live in now. My mom and Mrs. Campbell were good friends. They had six girls. Most were older than me. Anita Campbell was a grade ahead of me in school. We played together a lot. I don't ever remember any of the sisters disappearing."

Gully offered a suggestion, "We could look at old newspapers to see if anything like that happened. Do you remember any of their names?"

"Anita, of course, the one closest to me in age. The oldest was named Audrey. I remember her name because she was named after my ma. Help me, Joan. Can you recall any names?"

"Let me think a minute."

Walt looked at Bev, "Was there one named Edith?"

"I think there was. How did you come up with that name?"

Walt looked sheepishly at Joan, "I dated her a couple of times. I do know what became of her. She married a pig farmer in Dessison Township. Last I heard she had eight or ten kids."

Joan spoke up, "I think I know who you mean. I've seen her at some camp meetings. We need to keep her in mind. She would be the one to know what became of her sisters."

"That's good thinking Joan." Gully looked at his wife and nodded, "Let's go on. Is there anything you remember about the Campbells?"

"Yes, Mr. Campbell had a terrible accident. He had used horses for plowing up until about 1917 or '18, when he bought a tractor. He was the first farmer in the county to own a gas-powered tractor. The family was quite well-to-do.

"No one knows for sure what happened but somehow, he fell off his tractor and it fell on top of him. When he didn't come in for supper and it started to get dark, Mrs. Campbell and the girls went looking for him. One of the girls found him dead."

"Luella."

"What did you say Joan?" asked Walt.

"The daughter who found her father was Luella. She was the youngest, only about six or eight. I remember because my mom said that she was never right afterwards."

"Could she be the girl in the attic?" questioned Walt. "I wonder what became of her?"

"We're getting ahead of ourselves. Let's just concentrate on the time line and names. We'll investigate their whereabouts next." Gully was a very logical person.

"So, we have Anita, Audrey, Edith and Luella. There should be two more." Joan looked over at Bev and ticked the names off as she went down the list. "I'm sure the other names will come to us. Let's do as Gully suggested and make a time line for who lived in the house and when it was empty. The Campbells moved in when it was first built, about 1890. I know that Mrs. Campbell and the girls, who were not married, moved away a few months after Mr. Campbell died. Do you know how many were still living at home when the accident happened Bev? Or where they moved to?"

"I remember going to at least three weddings, maybe four. Probably two girls moved with Mrs. Campbell. I know Anita moved because I missed her so. Luella was probably the other daughter who went with Mrs. Campbell. Let's hope we can find out Edith's married name and get information about her sisters."

"What year did they move out Bev?"

"I know they didn't stay in the house for very long after the accident. Mrs. Campbell couldn't abide living there any longer. My dad farmed her land until Walt's brother, Steve, bought the place when he came back from the war."

"That's not exactly right. My brother came back in March of 1919. He and his wife Laura were living with us for a while. When Laura's dad passed that summer, she inherited quite a sum of money. They used the money to buy the farm from Mrs.

Campbell and moved in just after the new year of 1920."

Joan became excited, "The house sat empty from sometime in 1918 until January of 1920. Something ominous could have happened during that time, right Walt?"

"Well, yes, but don't you think Steve would have checked the attic when he moved in?"

"Did you check our attic when we moved in?"

"No. I have since. I would have seen a skeleton by now."

"Maybe Steve never went up into his attic."

"I guess anything is possible."

Bev diplomatically interrupted her friends' conversation, "Let's review and continue. The Campbell family lived in the house from about 1890 to 1918. It was empty from 1918 to 1920. When did Steve move out Walt?"

"Steve's life has been a sad one. He and Laura lived in the house from 1920 to 1936. They had two children: Michael born in December 1919, while living with us; Barbara born in December of the next year.

"When Barbara was sixteen, she fell down the basement stairs and broke her neck. Laura was so grief-stricken, she just wasted away and died about six months later."

"I remember. That was so sad," whispered Bev.

Walt continued, "Steve didn't want to live in the house any longer. He and Mike moved to town, in the house Steve still lives in. When the Second World War started, Mike enlisted in the Army Air Corps. He was killed in a training accident before he ever saw action. Steve is now a hurting old hermit who seems to hate everyone and everything."

Gully spoke up, "What a sad story! Is there any way possible the skeleton could be that of his daughter, Barbara or his wife?"

Joan answered, "Not very likely. I helped prepare both bodies for burial and was in the room when the caskets were shut."

Walt added, "And I helped carry the caskets to the grave sites. They were in there unless someone had taken one of the bodies out and replaced it with rocks, which I think is very unlikely."

Gully got up to refill his coffee cup, "Okay, we can cross them off the list of possibilities. Did your brother rent or sell the house?"

"No, he continued to farm the land. The house sat empty until 1950 when our son, Lou and his wife, Judy, moved in."

"That means from 1936 until 1950, it was unoccupied! I'll bet that's when the body got put up there," voiced Bev. "I think we should concentrate on women who went missing between those years."

"Hon, you might be right. I still think it will behoove us to account for all the Campbell sisters. Can any of you think of other women who went missing from this area over the past fifty years?

Walt spoke up, "I remember a couple drowning in Drayton Lake on Independence Day, 1918. I remember so well because it was just before I reported to Detroit for my Army induction physical. The fellow who drowned was to report with me. His name was Joel Thornton. I don't remember the girl's name. Neither body was ever recovered!"

"Yes, I remember that also," concurred Joan. "There was a picnic at the county park. Oh, how I remember that picnic! The Fourth that year fell on a Thursday and it had rained something awful most of the first part of the week. The picnic was almost called off. However, several men were leaving for Detroit Sunday afternoon to be inducted into the Army. And the town wanted to give them a good send-off. Drayton Lake was over its banks. That is the only time that I can remember the lake being that high. My mother was beside herself trying to set out food and watch my little brother. I was sixteen and wanted to be with my friends. Mom made me take my brother with me. It was mortifying."

Gully laughed, "What happened?"

Walt continued the tale his wife had started, "Joel and I had graduated from high school the year before. He worked at his dad's saw mill. He was really upset when he got the draft notice. He asked his dad to get him out of going. He thought working at the mill should get him deferred. He also had this girlfriend a couple of years younger than him and didn't want to leave her."

Joan picked up the story from her husband, "Her name was Jennifer Mitcham. She was a year ahead of me in high school. She and Joel wanted to get married before he left. Her dad said 'no'. They could wait until Joel got back.

"Towards the end of the picnic several people decided to get in row boats to watch the fireworks from the middle of the lake. You remember Walt? My dad wouldn't let us. He said the lake was too rough and we might capsize."

"Sure, I remember. I don't think he was so afraid of our capsizing as he was of my trying to make out with you in the boat."

"Well, my dad was probably right. Your trying to make out with me might have capsized the boat!" Everyone laughed at Joan's remark.

"Anyway, Joel and Jennifer went out in one of the boats and were never seen again. Like Walt said, their bodies were never found; although, the sunken boat was found with a large hole in the side."

"How far is the Hunt house from Drayton Lake?" questioned Gully.

Walt answered, "The lake is not near the house. However, a couple of creeks flow into the lake and only Drayton River flows out. It runs about a quarter mile behind the house."

Gully continued, "Listen to this scenario. The two planned a final tryst before Joel shipped out. They rowed down the river and pulled ashore near the house, knowing no one would be there. Something could have happened and Jenifer was accidentally killed. Joel panicked and hid her body in the attic and ran away. What do you think about that Walt?"

"That's a real possibility. Joel always thought a little better of himself than he should have. How do we go about proving it?"

"We'll have to find Joel." The four sat around the table looking at each other.

Bev had been taking notes on their discussion when her eyes lit up. "Gully, do you remember the name of the lawyer who represented the sellers of our home?"

Gully looked at her for a second than said, "Thornton. Do you think he might be related to Joel Thornton?"

"We should find out."

"Walt, tomorrow how about you and me go…"

Bev interrupted her husband, "Now dear, you can't go tomorrow. Remember your sister and Earl are coming in tomorrow to visit for the weekend."

"Rats! I forgot. Earl, my sister's husband, and I don't see eye-to-eye. He has some really weird ideas. I can hardly stand to be around the man. He and Monica have been married over fifty years. She's a saint. I guess we'll have to go after their visit. Maybe you can find out the lawyer's address.

Walt looked at his wife, "Joan, reach me the telephone book."

Joan got the book and handed it to Walt. He thumbed through the book, then said, "Here is a Richard Thornton in Wellington. Joel was from Wellington. That's probably the right man. Do you want me to call for an appointment?"

"No, let's just show up. The shock effect will be worth it."

Bev continued taking notes, "I left to marry Gully in 1925. Is there any other woman you two remember mysteriously disappearing since then?"

"There was one." As Joan said this, she looked at Walt. "You remember don't you Walt, Mike's fiancé? As Walt said earlier, Mike, Steve's son, was killed in pilot training in 1942. He had a fiancé named Alice Higgins. She wasn't from here. I think she originally came from Indiana. Alice had a widowed aunt who lived on Pine Street. The aunt was ill and Alice was a nurse, so she came to help care for her. Alice also got a job at the county hospital. Mike was working part-time there while going to the junior college. They met and fell in love."

"Yeah, weren't they planning on a wedding when he came home on his first leave?"

Joan nodded at her husband and continued, "When Mike died, his body was brought back for burial. Alice came to the funeral and sat at the back of the church. We asked her to come and sit with the family but she wouldn't. The community had a dinner after the graveside service. Alice didn't go to the cemetery or the meal. No one ever saw her again."

"Is her aunt still alive? Would she know what happened to Alice?"

"No Bev. Her aunt died in the fall of 1941, before the start of the war."

Gully asked, "What about someone at the hospital? It seems this Alice would have given notice of leaving."

"Harriet Seymour might remember her. She's Judy's mother. Before the war, Mrs. Seymour worked as a nurse at the hospital."

Gully looked at Joan in dismay, "Judy and

Lou have been married for how many years, and you still call her mother Mrs.!"

Joan smiled, "Me and Mrs. Seymour aren't on the best of terms. She didn't want Judy to marry Lou. She felt Judy was marrying beneath her."

Walt broke in, "Mrs. 'High-and-Mighty' thought our Lou wasn't good enough for her Judy."

"Walt, be nice. Before the war, the Seymours lived in a small house here in Leichester. Martin Seymour made a lot of money during the war. About 1948, his wife insisted they move to a better place. They built that big yellow brick house with the blue shutters on Mill's End Road."

Walt leaned over to Joan and put his arm around her shoulders, "Judy's mother, Harriet, wanted Judy to marry some hot-shot executive at her dad's company. At first Harriet said she wouldn't even come to Lou's and Judy's wedding." Walt smiled and squeezed his wife's shoulder then continued, "Joan telephoned Harriet and put a bug in her ear."

Bev asked, "So I take it Joan, you would not be comfortable asking Mrs. Seymour about Mike's girlfriend?"

"Not really, nevertheless, I'll talk to Judy about her asking her mom about Jennifer."

"Anyone else you can think of Joan?"

"No Bev, I can't. Can you Walt?"

"No, this is a small community. Everyone just about knows everybody else's business."

"All right, let's review." Gully looked at Bev, "Read over your notes, Sweet."

"The house with the skeleton was built about 1890. Mr. and Mrs. Campbell and their six daughters lived there until 1918. It sat empty until Steve Hunt and his family moved in, in 1920, moving out in 1936. Then no one lived in the place until 1950."

Bev turned the page and continued reading, "Verify the following: whereabouts of the six Campbell daughters. I'll do that. I have an idea how to go about doing it. Next, what happened to Jennifer Mitcham?"

Gully raised his hand as though he were in school, "Walt and I can handle that one."

Last is Mike Hunt's girlfriend, Alice Higgins." Bev looked at Joan, "Are you sure you want to investigate her?"

"Yes, like I said, I'll get Judy to help me."

"Bev, we need to get going. Y'know, this may turn out to be very interesting."

The Gullingtons left soon afterwards. Walt sat in his favorite chair and was soon snoring. Joan was cleaning up the kitchen when the telephone rang. It was Judy to let her know the roads were open so the children would be riding the bus home. "Good", thought Joan. She was rather weary from the day's activities.

When Joan was finished with the kitchen, she sat at the table thumbing through a cookbook. Joan had a large collection of cookbooks even though Walt didn't care for much variety in his meals. He was satisfied with fried chicken and potatoes, fried fish and french fries, fried pork chops and potatoes, and roast beef with mashed potatoes and gravy. Joan didn't complain; he was an easy man to cook for. She enjoyed reading the various books and looking at the pictures

Chapter 9

Darlene startled Joan as she came through the kitchen door. Joan looked up at the clock. She was surprised to see it was almost four. "What are you doing here? Your mom said you would be riding the bus home."

"I missed the bus."

Walt came walking into the kitchen, "Hi Sugar, where are the other kids?"

"They rode the bus home. I missed it."

Joan looked at her granddaughter suspiciously, "How did that happen?"

"Well, I sort of had to stay after school."

"Sit down. Joan, fetch Darlene some milk and something to eat."

"All I have are graham crackers."

"I like graham crackers," said Darlene as she slid into a chair. "I'd better call Mom. She'll wonder where I am. Will you take me home Grampa?"

"Sure Sugar. Now tell us what happened."

After first calling home, Darlene then took a swallow of milk, "I forgot that Mrs. Fuller, the English teacher, told us to memorize some stupid poem. The test on it was last week. While all the other kids were writing it down, I just sat there like a fool. After class I asked Mrs. Fuller, real nice, what I could do to make-up for the F. She said to memorize that poem plus one more."

Darlene paused to eat a cracker and drink some more milk. "I did just what she said. I even picked a long poem to show her how sorry I was. Grandpa, it was a poem by Robert Frost. Have you ever heard of him?"

"Of course, I've heard of him. He just died a couple of years ago. I think we have a book of his poems."

"The poem I memorized is '**The Witch of Coös.**' It's about a skeleton that walked up from a basement to the attic. Then the witch had her husband nail the door to the attic shut and put their bed in front of the door. At night they could hear the skeleton walking down the stairs, wondering why he couldn't get out. Doesn't that sound almost like our skeleton?"

"Sugar, it sure does. But I thought our skeleton was a woman?"

"It had a dress on. So, it probably was a woman. Anyway, today Mrs. Fuller checked the poems I memorized. I didn't have one mistake! Then I saw her write a red C in her grade book. I asked what that meant. She said, 'credit'. I asked wasn't she going to erase the 'F'. She said, 'Oh no! Grades can never be erased.'I told her it wasn't fair; I thought memorizing two poems would cancel out the 'F'. I guess I kinda yelled and maybe said some other things. Anyway, she sent me to the office.

"The principal was busy so I had to wait. He never asked to see me. Finally, I asked when I was going to get to see the principal. The secretary said I was so quiet, she forgot about me. By then the bus had left and the principal had never come back from his appointment. She said he must have gone on home." Tears started rolling down Darlene's cheeks as she finished her narrative. "It's not fair Grampa. It's just not fair."

Walt wrapped his granddaughter in his big arms and patted her on her back, "There, there, Sugar, life isn't always fair. We often get hurt, even when we try to do the right thing." Walt looked at Joan as if to say, "Help me here!"

Joan got up and kissed Darlene on the forehead. "Grandpa will take you home. You tell your parents what happened. See what they say."

Grandpa took his handkerchief from his back pocket, "Here, take this hanky and wipe your face."

As the car disappeared down the road

Joan sighed and was glad her four children were grown.

Judy listened quietly as Darlene miserably retold her misadventure. Judy sighed, not for the first time, at her daughter. Judy had been a student of Mrs. Fuller and remembered her as a very strict teacher. She did wonder about Mrs. Fuller's logic regarding her grading.

The next day Judy dropped Gloria off at Joan's. Darlene's parents had an appointment with Mrs. Fuller for after school. Lou was to meet her at the high school. Judy was surprised, Lou had agreed to leave work early. He normally let Judy handle any school problems.

Mrs. Fuller greeted them at the main entrance. Darlene stood beside her. "I thought we could have our little conference in the library. It will be more comfortable than you trying to fit into a desk."

 Darlene, Judy and Lou followed in silence as they made their way to the library. Lou was still a little intimidated and unnerved by Mrs. Fuller. He had spent more than one time in the principal's office for getting into trouble in her class.

When the four were seated Mrs. Fuller asked, "What is it you want to discuss with me?"

Judy had thought a long time about what she was going to say. She began, "We understand Darlene is at fault for not memorizing a poem. She told us, however, that you told her if she memorized that poem, plus one more, you would erase the 'F'."

"What Darlene told you is not exactly

correct. She asked me if there was something she could do to make up for not knowing the poem. I told her to memorize the poem plus one more, which she did. And I've given her credit for doing so."

Lou had been sitting mutely listening. He couldn't keep quiet any longer and stated, "Well, what good did that do?"

Mrs. Fuller gave him a stern look that silenced him. "At the end of the grading term if her grade is very close between, say a 'B' or a 'C', then I would give her the 'B'.

"Hmm, it will be more likely between a 'D' and an 'F'," put in Darlene.

Mrs. Fuller turned her full attention to Darlene, "At least you would pass. I'd like to add Darlene, you are a very bright girl. There is no reason you should be getting such low grades. Your memorizing those two poems so quickly shows that you are intelligent. If you would get better organized, such as keeping an assignment notebook, to help you remember your homework, you could achieve much more."

Darlene seemed not to have heard anything Mrs. Fuller had said, "What if I'm right in the middle of a grade with no chance of getting enough points to move up? What good will the "credit" do?"

Mrs. Fuller sighed, "None." Having said this, she reached for her grade book and changed the 'F' into a 'B'. She showed it to Darlene and her parents, "Will this make you a better student?"

The three looked at Mrs. Fuller. Darlene smiled, "It does make me feel better. But it probably won't make me a better student."

Mrs. Fuller got up and stated, "I believe this conference is finished."

Lou drove over to his folks to pick up Gloria. She would be over the moon to ride home in Daddy's truck. Judy and Darlene headed home to prepare supper. "I don't understand why Mrs. Fuller told me to memorize two poems when it wasn't going to change anything."

"I think she didn't expect you would bother memorizing the poems and that would have put an end to the situation."

"Well, I showed her. Didn't I?"

"Yes, you did. It also shows what you are capable of. You are not dumb. In fact, you are very smart. With a little more effort, you could be a very good student."

"I don't like school and I don't like to study. I just want to have fun."

"God wants us to be happy and enjoy life. However, He also expects us to have a purpose for being alive. My grandfather once told me that every person should strive to live in such a way that others will remember the good that he or she did. What do you think you want to be… to do… when you grow up?"

"I really don't know."

"Have you given any thought to the electives you're going to take next year?"

"Yes, I'm taking Business Math and Wood Shop."

"How on earth did you come up with those?"

"Mom, you're always telling us to pray about things before we do anything. So, I prayed and God told me to sign up for Business Math and Wood Shop."

Judy stared at her daughter and almost ran the car into a ditch.

At the end of the semester Darlene would earn a 'C+' in English. The school counselor would not let her take Wood Shop. She said it was only open for boys and suggested Darlene take Home Economics. Darlene, having no interest in Home Economics, signed up for Typing instead.

Lou told Darlene if she was really interested in learning about tools and fixing things, he would teach her. After this, Darlene worked with her dad repairing things around the house and even helping him work on the car.

Chapter 10

A week passed before Walt and Gully were able to get together for their trip to Wellington. It was close to noon when they arrived at Richard Thornton's office on the second floor of the Wellington Community Bank building. His office comprised the entire second floor. The secretary told them they needed an appointment to see Mr. Thornton. They created such a ruckus that Richard came from his office to see what was going on. He was about Gully's age, sixty-five. Unlike Gully he was over-weight and by the look of his eyes and bulbous nose appeared to bend his elbow frequently.

"See here. What's all the noise?"

"Mr. Thornton, these two gentlemen insist on seeing you. However, they don't have an appointment."

Gully interrupted her, "We just want to ask you a couple of questions about Joel Thornton. It won't take more than a few minutes. Are you related to him?"

"My brother Joel? He's been dead for years. You have no right coming in like this, so leave now before I call the authorities."

"We're helping the sheriff's office with an investigation. Please just let us talk with you. We only have a couple of questions." Walter Hunt was a calmer man than Gully and tried to quiet down the situation.

"I said to get out of here before I call the sheriff."

Walt grabbed Gully's arm, pulling him towards the door. "Okay, okay we're leaving. Come on Gully."

Back in the car Gully was still fuming. "Boy! What a jerk he is! I'll bet you, he knows something."

"Well, for sure, he's not going to tell us. Are you hungry? I am. Let's find a place for lunch."

At the edge of town, they came to a small diner. It looked like an old train car. It sat on what appeared to be an abandoned rail siding. Once inside, they sat in a booth and ordered lunch. The diner wasn't very busy so when their waitress, Louise, brought their order, Walt engaged her in conversation. "Have you worked here long?"

"I'll say I have! Next month it'll be fifteen years."

"So, you must have lived in Wellington a long time."

"All my life, I know just about everyone in town. It's the first time I've seen you two, though."

"We're from Leichester. You ever been there?"

"Oh, I've gone through it a time or two. I used to know some people there, but they moved."

Gully entered the conversation, "Say, if you've lived here all your life, you might know some people we're trying to find."

"I probably do. What's their name?"

"Mitcham."

"There are a number of Mitchams living here. As a matter-of-fact, Mitcham is my grandmother's maiden name."

"Do you know if she is related to a Jennifer Mitcham?"

Louise stood staring at the two men for several seconds. Finally, she asked, "Why would you be asking about her?"

Gully lied, "We're helping the sheriff's office with an investigation."

Louise looked at Gully and said, "Let me make a phone call."

Once Louise had left their table, Walt chastised his friend, "Gully, you're going to get us in trouble making people think we're working for the sheriff."

"Well, we are, in a way. They're so

shorthanded just now. How much effort do you think they're putting into solving this case?"

As Gully was talking, the door opened and Deputy Sheriff Sean O'Toole walked in. He stopped, looked around, spied the men and walked over to their booth. Leaning over the table and putting his hands on it he asked, "Just what have you gentlemen been up to?"

Gully answered him, "Eating lunch. Sit down; we'll buy you a hamburger. They're really good."

"I'm not here to eat. The Sheriff got a complaint from one Richard Thornton. A lawyer, mind you! He claims you were harassing him. He maintains you told him, you two are working for the department. The sheriff sent me to find you. Is what Mr. Thornton said true?"

Walt meekly answered, "We went to see him, yes. We sure didn't mean to harass him. We're only trying to help the sheriff find out who the skeleton is. We know you're short staffed with that robbery and the deputy that got injured. We're only trying to help. Honest!"

"You could go to jail for impersonating an officer of the law. So, cease and desist."

Just then Louise returned to their table. "Deputy, are you eating?"

Before Sean could answer Gully ordered for him, "Sure he is. Bring him a cheeseburger and some fries. O'Toole, sit down."

Louise looked at Sean, "Do you want everything on it?"

Sean sighed and sat down. "No onions. Oh, and Louise, bring me a cup of coffee."

Before going to put in Sean's order, Louise addressed Walt and Gully, "My grandma lives with my mom. She said to come over this afternoon and she'll see you. Here's the address." Louise went to the kitchen window to place Sean's order.

"See there O'Toole! We're making progress," Gully triumphantly smirked. "Say, how did you know the waitress's name was Louise?"

"I saw her name on the tag of her blouse."

"Yeah, I noticed that blouse too." The three men laughed.

While Sean ate his cheeseburger, Walt explained to him about Jennifer Mitcham. Sean told the men to give him the paper containing the address of Louise's grandmother. He then asked, "What was that business with the lawyer?"

Gully explained, "We're trying to find out about all the people that lived in the area and may have disappeared."

On leaving the diner, Sean told the older men to follow him and gave them strict orders, "Once we get there, I'll do the questioning. Neither of you say anything. Agreed?" Both nodded.

The house was an older two-story frame home. The lawn was well kept with a border of early blooming yellow jonquils on either side of the front steps. A middle-aged woman answered their knock. "Good afternoon, Officers. I'm Muriel Freed, Louise's mother."

"Hello Mrs. Freed. Thank you for seeing us. I'm Deputy Sean O'Toole. These gentlemen are not with the department. They're just interested parties."

"Please come in. This is my mother, Mrs. Pauline Mitcham Taylor." Mrs. Taylor was seated in an overstuffed chair. Her hair was light blue and very curly. She had on a faded pink house dress, white ankle socks and tennis shoes. "Please sit down. Mother, this is Deputy O'Toole and…? "

"I'm sorry; this is Henry Gullington and Walter Hunt. Thank you Mrs. Taylor, for agreeing to this interview. The sheriff's department is trying to close some old cases on the books. One is the disappearance of Jennifer Mitcham who disappeared at the same time as Joel Thornton. We're hoping you can shed some light on what happened."

"My goodness, the sheriff must not have much to do if he's spending time solving fifty-year-old missing person's cases."

"That's not exactly true. A skeleton was

found near Leichester several days ago. We're trying to identify it."

"Well, it's not Jennifer. I know that for a fact."

"How do you know Mrs. Taylor?"

She did not say anything at first. Looking at her daughter then Gully, then Walt, and finally settling her pale blue eyes on Sean, "I guess it won't hurt to let the truth be told now." She paused briefly before continuing. "Please understand what I'm going to tell you, I only learned a little over a year ago.

"In 1918, my sister Jennifer was sixteen. She and Joel, he was nineteen, were dating. Joel was so full of himself. He was really handsome with dark wavy hair and very dark eyes. He was tall and slim and had been the star on the football team as well as the basketball and track teams. Jennifer was so smitten with him. She couldn't see how self-centered and conceited he was. She was kind of plain looking with pale eyes, like mine, and stringy dish-water brown hair. At the time, I thought he only went with her because she made him look more handsome.

"The Great War was on and Joel received his draft notice. They went to my father and asked permission to marry. My father would not give permission or sign for Jennifer to wed. He said they should wait a year. What they didn't tell him was that she was pregnant. I believe if they had, he of course would have wanted them to get married.

"Since they couldn't legally marry, they concocted a plan to run away. A couple of days before the Fourth of July, there was a terrible storm. Several tree limbs were blown down. This fit right into their plan.

"On the Fourth, they went to a celebration held at the Drayton County Park. Just before dusk they told everyone they were going to take a boat ride down the Drayton River to watch the fireworks. The river was high and swift from the rain. They rowed to where they had hidden some supplies." Mrs. Taylor paused and looked out a window as if collecting her thoughts before continuing.

"Joel put Jennifer ashore, took an axe and a fallen tree limb, then rowed to the center of the river. He chopped a hole in the boat, shoved the limb through it, then jumped overboard and swam to shore. Their hope was the boat would be found. People would believe they had drowned when the boat was impaled by the limb and sank."

Looking intently at Sean, she tightened her lips and made fists with each hand. Then she visibly relaxed and resumed her story. "They made their way to Detroit, then took a bus to Indianapolis. Joel had worked in his father's saw mill here in Wellington and was able to get a job at a local lumber yard. They changed their names and lied about their ages to get married. They lived in Indianapolis as Joel and Jennifer Langston for the rest of their lives. They had three children who never knew the truth about them." Mrs. Taylor stopped as if exhausted. After taking a drink of water she continued.

"Last year a man knocked at my door. I knew instantly who he was. He was the exact image of Joel. I knew right then the two hadn't drowned. They just ran away! He said he was my nephew and that his mother, my sister, was in the car. He was polite enough and asked if I would agree to see her. I was reluctant at first because I was furious. But I was also very curious. I told him to have her come in. He had to carry her. She was pitiful to behold. Arthritis had crippled her horribly. Her hands looked like claws and her legs were bent close to her body. Joel was dead, having died about five years earlier of a heart attack. She told me the story I have just related to you."

Walt was leaning forward listening intently, "Did your sister say why she never contacted you earlier?"

"She said Joel was afraid he would go to prison for not going into the Army. Joel was a coward. No man wants to fight or kill. No mother or wife wants her loved one to die. My husband served in the Great War and my two boys both served in the last one. One was wounded and spent months in the hospital. My younger one was in a Japanese prison camp for eight months. He still has nightmares about that time. My boys were not cowards! Joel was a coward!"

"Mother, calm yourself! Please don't get so excited."

"I'm sorry. It just makes me so angry when I think about those two." She took another deep breath and sighed.

"My sister died soon after visiting me. Her son asked me to come to the funeral. I did. Nonetheless, I had no tears for her. I shed my tears fifty years ago. That's when she died to me. Her maiden name was not even put in the obituary or on the tombstone. Just Jennifer Langston."

Sean took Mrs. Taylor's hand, "Thank you

for giving us this information. I know it wasn't easy for you. It does help in our investigation."

Gully asked, "Do you know if Richard Thornton or any of his family know about your sister and his brother?"

Sean gave him a warning stare.

"Yes, that scoundrel does. He helped them get away. Where do you think they got the axe? He's the one that drove them to Detroit. He even visited them in Indianapolis several times over the years. All the time my folks were grieving for their lost daughter, and he knew the truth!"

"Mother! Please, try to calm down. There isn't anything that can be done now. Nothing can change what's happened."

Sean stood up and motioned for Walt and Gully to do the same, "We're sorry to have upset you Mrs. Taylor. We'll be leaving. This is my card in case you want to contact me. Thank you again for talking to us and sharing this information."

Chapter 11

The rains of April brought the promised flowers to May. Len Rheimes, the only remaining thief from the Smitty burglary, walked along a small creek. Toward dark he came to a farm. Lights were on in several rooms. Len could hear people talking. A great sadness overcame him as he sat down and started throwing stones into the creek. "I've always been an outsider. My ma had even tried to get rid of me before I was born."

He remembered as a youngster listening to his mother, aunt and grandma talking.

His aunt was crying and repeating some terrible things his uncle had said when his aunt had told him she was expecting their eighth child. Len heard his grandma say something to the aunt that he didn't understand. His mother laughed and added, "Oh, that's what you told me to do when I was pregnant with Leonard. It didn't work because Leonard still got born."

When he was older, he realized they were talking about abortion. His mother had tried to abort him! He never felt his mother really loved him. It seemed whatever he tried to do; his mother would put him down. His father made good money which Len sometimes stole. His dad never had much time for his son.

He wasn't really liked at school either, always feeling inferior and getting into trouble. At the age of sixteen Len had quit school, wandering from one odd job to another. At eighteen, despite not having a high school diploma, the Army drafted him. There in the service he felt confident and good about himself for the first time in his life. "I should have stayed in the Army," he thought for at least the 100th time.

While Len was ruing his past decisions, it was prom season at the high school. Jimmy Palmer, a senior, asked Betty to be his date to the prom even though she was only a sophomore. She didn't really care for Jimmy. They had never dated before. However, to be asked to the prom as a sophomore was something special. Very few sophomore girls ever got to go.

The Saturday morning of the prom Judy dropped Betty off at Mavis Hampton's beauty salon, Tangles. Betty opened the front door and was assaulted by a cacophony of teen-aged girls' voices. Mavis' salon was in a small, remodeled old house on Main Street. Along the north side of the living room were two hair dryers, both occupied. Facing the dryers on the other side of the room sat Valerie Smith with a towel wrapped around her wet hair. She was the only other sophomore, Betty had heard about, who was going to the prom. In another chair sat Pauline Ermantrout talking to Lisa Miller. Lisa had curlers in her hair and was waiting to go under a dryer as soon as one became available. Two seniors, Noel Johnson and Abby Saunders stood off to the side discussing some picture in a magazine.

A third of the dining room had been partitioned to make a shampoo area. Two wash bowls lined the partition. Across from the wash bowls Peggy Mulholland sat in Mavis' styling chair. Mavis was just putting the finishing touches to Peggy's hair. Several colors of cut hair lay on the floor at her feet.

Mavis looked at Betty and pursed her lips before saying, "Come on in Betty. I'm behind as you can see. It's going to be awhile. The electricity was out for an hour this morning. Someone said a car hit a pole."

"Yeah, and it didn't help that Monica Andrews didn't like how her hair looked and fussed until Mavis redid it." This bit of information was volunteered by Wanda Evans as she lifted the dryer, she was sitting under, which had just turned off.

Judy had taught her daughters not to stand around if there was work to be done. She would have been very proud of Betty this morning. "Where's the broom? I'll sweep up this hair before it gets tracked all over."

"Oh Betty, that sure would be helpful. It's in the corner, over there," Mavis pointed with her rat-tailed comb.

When Betty had the hair swept up, she asked, "Would you like me to take the curlers out of Wanda's hair? Her dryer has stopped."

Mavis nodded, "First put Lisa under for thirty minutes. Thanks."

When Betty had the curlers out of Wanda's hair, she told Mavis, "I wash my little sisters' hair all the time. Would you like me to wash one of the girl's hair?"

"Thanks, yes, do Pauline's first."

Betty stayed the rest of the day, having called Judy to tell her what happened. Mavis said she would drive Betty home when they were finished and gave

Betty a free cut and style and even did her make-up.

Betty sat in the styling chair and watched as Mavis expertly fashioned her hair into a French twist.

Mavis was twenty-eight, a bottle blond with an hour glass figure. She had arrived in Leichester five years ago. No one knew where she was from or anything about her background. Somehow the rumor spread around town that she was divorced. One of the very few "divorced women" anyone in town had ever met! Betty thought Mavis was the most sophisticated woman in town. "Mavis, may I ask you a personal question?"

"Sure, if I don't like it, I just won't answer." Both laughed.

"Do you think you'll ever get married again?"

"Again! I haven't been married the first time yet."

"You haven't? Everyone thinks you're divorced."

"Well, I can't help what everyone thinks. The man I would have married died in the Korean War."

"That's awful. What was his name?"

"Oh, I never met him."

"You never met him? You said he was the man you were going to marry!"

"No, I said he was the man I would have married. We never met. I'm sure one of those 36,000 men who died over there would have come home, we would have met, fallen in love and married."

Betty gazed in the mirror at Mavis, "How did you happen to come to Leichester?"

"I didn't just happen to come to Leichester. This house was my great aunt's, my mom's aunt. She gave it to me in her will."

"Where are you from?"

"I grew up in the thumb, just west of Caseville. My dad was a veterinarian."

"Did you get to help him?"

"Did I get to help! I'll say I did. That's why I don't have any pets now. They're a big responsibility."

"I know. People are always dropping off unwanted pets out by our place in the country. At one time, we had twelve cats and seven dogs."

"What happened to them?"

Betty hesitated before answering, "My dad shot most of them. He said it was too dangerous having them around with all of us kids. He was afraid the animals would bite one of us or give us some disease. I wish people were more responsible about animals.

"A few weeks ago, a kitten jumped through a broken window in my brother, Louis's bedroom. It had to be killed and tested for rabies. Thankfully it didn't have rabies." She was silent before going on, "Does your dad still run his clinic?"

"Not really, I have an older brother who went to vet college. He and his wife, who is also a vet, now do most of the work. My dad only helps out now and then. He's kind of a consultant for difficult cases."

"You never wanted to become a vet?"

"I've always liked fussing with hair. My mother would sit and let me fix her hair in the evenings while we watched TV. I just always wanted to be a beautician. After high school I went to beauty school then worked in a salon in Bay City until I got this house."

"Your great aunt must have really liked you to leave you a whole house."

"My Aunt Amanda, my great aunt, and her husband Irving Steel moved to this house soon after they were married in the early 1920s. I never knew my aunt's husband. My Aunt Amanda said her husband was very secretive about his job. She really never knew what he did. It was not unusual for men to come to their house to talk business with him. At those times, Uncle Irving would give her some money and tell her to go shopping for a couple of hours. She said sometimes he would leave and be gone for days at a time. I think she knew he was into something illegal. It was during

Prohibition, the time in the U. S. when selling alcohol was illegal.

"She told me, one day two burly looking men came to the house. They asked to see my uncle and told her to scram. She only walked down to the corner to where she could watch the house. Her husband came out of the house between the men. He saw her standing next to a fence and shook his head at her. She said he looked really scared. She never saw him again. After waiting two days, she reported him missing to the sheriff. They just took her report, and didn't give her any information."

"Did your aunt ever learn what happened to him?"

"Well, about a week later, two FBI men came asking questions. They went through my uncle's desk and took all his papers. Then they went down into the basement and brought up several cases of Canadian whiskey. She said that she had no idea there was alcohol in the house. The FBI men left and wouldn't give her any information. They even went to my folks and asked them if they knew anything about Uncle Irving. I really think my dad might have, although, he wouldn't tell them anything.

The next month when Aunt Amanda balanced her checkbook, there was an extra hundred dollars in it. Now this was the depression and a hundred dollars was a lot of money. Every month from then on, extra money was always in her account and it increased monthly as the years went by. She worried the "mob" was sending it and was afraid to say anything to the authorities.

"When I was growing up, I used to come

here to visit. She was really a nice person. We would go to the best places. She took me to the Detroit Art Museum once. On the way back she got really sleepy and I had to talk to her all the way home. I asked her the most ridiculous stuff, just to keep her talking." Both of them laughed.

"As she aged, I started visiting her more often. I came every few months at first. Then later I would come about every Monday on my day off. I'd perm or cut her hair, take her to buy groceries, or to a doctor's appointment, things like that. When she died, she left me this house. It took me several months before it went through probate. Then several more months remodeling it before I could open it as Tangles."

"Did the FBI ever come back and tell your aunt why they were interested?"

"No, she figured he was mixed up with the mob. He must have displeased them somehow and they rubbed him out. She never found out what happened to him or what his business was."

"Mavis, you've heard about the skeleton my sister and brother found in the attic, haven't you?"

"Sure, who hasn't? Are you thinking it might be Uncle Irving?"

"Yes!"

"I thought the skeleton was a woman?"

"Well, it had lace material around it, that could have been a dress. Couldn't the killers have put a dress on him to confuse the sheriff? I think you should go see Sheriff Byrne and tell him about your uncle."

"Hmmm, maybe I should. I'll be closed on Monday. I'll go over then. To change the subject, Betty you were a real help today. How would you like to come to work for me? It would only be very part-time. I could use you on most Saturday mornings and on special days, like before a big holiday."

"Oh, Mavis, I would love to!"

Chapter 12

Betty returned home late in the afternoon and immediately started preparing for her big evening. Judy was out shopping. Darlene was off to one of her friend's. Gloria was taking her afternoon nap. Lou sat in his favorite chair doing the crossword puzzle from the Flint Journal. Suddenly, he heard Connie scream and then heard something come tumbling down the stairs. He jumped up and ran to the door leading to the stairs. As he opened it, a badly bent doll buggy toppled out onto the floor. He gazed up the stairs to see Connie coming down, loudly sobbing her heart out and holding her arm. At the top of the stairs stood Louis with a menacing scowl on his face. "What's going on?"

"Daddy, Louis hit me and threw my buggy down the stairs! Now look at it. It's broken to bits."

"Louis, come down here." Louis slowly walked down the steps until he stood behind his sister. "Both of you come into the dining room. Louis, bring the buggy. Now tell me what's going on. Why did you hit Connie and push her buggy down the stairs?"

Louis stood with his arms crossed and glared in anger at his sister. "I was trying to do my science project. It's due Monday. She was making so much racket in the hall that I couldn't think straight. I asked her twice to be quiet. She wouldn't shut up!"

"I wasn't making a racket! I was singing!"

"Okay Connie. You don't have to shout."

As Lou said this Gloria came down the stairs rubbing one eye and holding her teddy bear by its ear. "What's going on? Why is everybody yelling? Connie, what happened to your buggy?"

Lou heaved a long sigh, "Louis go get my tool box. Let's try to fix it." Louis gave Connie another sour look and clomped off. "Louis, you'd best change that attitude of yours!"

Lou knelt on one knee and began to straighten the buggy as much as he could. "This thing is pretty much shot. It sure has seen better days."

"It used to be Darlene's and before that it was Betty's. I'm getting quite old, I'm almost eight. I should probably give it to

Gloria." Connie said this as she and Gloria sat crossed legged on the floor watching their dad work.

"I don't want that old thing. I want a new one. I always get the stuff nobody else wants anymore. My teddy doesn't want to ride in a beat-up thing like that!"

Louis came back with the tool box. Together, father and son worked on straightening the buggy. Connie, not content to sit and watch, got up, picked up a small screw driver and began to poke the frame. Lou wasn't sure what she was supposed to be doing. Just then as Connie pushed the screw driver into a part of the buggy frame, it slipped and went into Lou's left thumb. Blood squirted out. Lou instinctively put the injured thumb to his lips and sucked on it. Gloria shot up from the floor and grabbed her dad around the neck.

"Daddy, you're hurt! Please don't die!"

"Gloria, it's only a small cut. I'm not going to die. Connie, do you know where Mom keeps the first aid kit?" Connie nodded. "Please go get it." Connie helped Lou put an adhesive bandage on his thumb. It immediately bled through. He took some black electrical tape from his tool box and wrapped it around his thumb on top of the bandage.

Connie shouted at Louis, "See what you caused! You mean brother! My buggy's broke and Daddy's hurt!" Gloria started crying.

Louis shouted at Gloria, "Why are you crying? You snot nosed baby!"

"Children, that's enough! Louis, go sit on

the pouting chair and face the wall. Be quiet and don't even breathe hard. Gloria why are you crying?"

"Because I'm sad. I want my mommy." Lou stood and looked at her thinking, "How does Judy ever do it? Day after day!"

Betty came out from her bedroom, "What's going on out here? Why all the commotion? This place is like a circus."

"Betty, take Gloria to your room and...do something with her."

"What! I'm trying to get ready for the prom."

"You heard me, don't argue."

"Come on child. You can look through one of my old teen magazines." Gloria was immediately placated because Betty normally yelled at her if she even touched one of those precious magazines.

Before Gloria left, she asked her dad, "Daddy, when you get a booboo who kisses it and makes it better?"

Lou looked at his sweet daughter with loving eyes, "Well, Honey, when a person grows up, I guess, he just has to kiss it himself."

Connie sat back down and watched her dad as he continued to work with the buggy until he had it straightened as much as he could. "Here you go Sugar. It's the best I can do."

"Thank you, Daddy. I'm sorry for hurting you. I was only trying to help."

"I know, I know. Next time, remember, if you don't know what you're doing, ask first.

"Louis, carry this back upstairs for your sister and be nice about it. Then come into the kitchen. We need to have a man-to-man talk."

The walk up the stairs and back down was one of the longest walks Louis could ever remember taking. What was a man-to-man talk anyway? He walked slowly into the kitchen as his dad was pouring a cup of coffee.

"Sit. This is the first of many man-to-man talks we're likely to have in the next several years. Would you like a cup of coffee?"

"I'm not sure I'm old enough to drink coffee."

"You'll be thirteen in two weeks. That's almost a man. I guess you're old enough. How about some sugar and milk in it?"

"You drink your coffee black, don't you?" Lou nodded. "Then I'll try mine black."

Lou brought two cups of black coffee to the table and sat down. He watched as Louis took a sip and grimaced. He pushed the sugar container towards Louis. "Here, put a little sugar in it. You'll probably like it better that way."

Lou took a deep breath and let out a sigh, "Louis, in just a few years you'll be a man. You'll be dating and before you know it, you'll be married with children of your own. There are many things you must learn. One of the first and most important is, a man never, never, never hits a woman. If he does, he's not a man. That includes your sisters."

"But Dad, Connie made me so mad! I asked her twice not to push that noisy thing back and forth in the hall. Her singing, if that's what it can be called, sounds like a cat howling. I couldn't think. I have to get my science project done by Monday."

"Nothing ever justifies a boy or man hitting a girl or woman. Nothing! You're learning how exasperating females can be. I love your mother more than anyone else in this world. Still there are times when I just don't understand her and I get very irritated with what she does. But I would never harm her.

"Women are to be cherished, loved and cared for by men. They are God's special gift to men. Even your sisters are God's gift to you. I expect you to look after them, not to hurt them. What could you have done besides hitting Connie and throwing the buggy down the stairs?"

Louis sat with his head down, his coffee getting cold. "Louis look at me. Think, what should you have done?"

Louis looked at his dad, "I guess I could have come downstairs and worked at the dining room table like Darlene does sometimes."

"That sure would have prevented a lot of grief and havoc. Tell me why you've waited until the last weekend to do this project anyway? How long have you known it was due this Monday?"

"You're right Dad. Mr. Close assigned the project two weeks ago."

Just then Connie came into the kitchen holding a wheel. She had one hand on her hip and held a wheel in the other, "The wheel fell off."

Lou looked at her and sighed. Louis spoke up before Lou could say anything. "Connie, I'm sorry I hit you and threw your buggy down the stairs. My birthday is in two weeks. If I get enough money, I'll buy you a new buggy."

Lou was so proud of his son; he thought his heart would burst.

Connie stood and considered what her brother had just said, before finally saying, "I thought you were going to buy a new baseball glove with your birthday money?"

"Well, I was. My old one will last another season."

Connie started to walk away then turned around. "Y'know, I really don't play with the buggy much anymore. I'm getting too big for it. I only kept making noise because I knew it was bothering you. I'm sorry. You don't have to buy me a buggy with your birthday money. Use it to get a glove."

Connie left and went into Betty's bedroom, much to Betty's annoyance. Lou and

Louis sat at the kitchen table staring at each other. Lou smiled, "Louis, I told you females are a strange lot. You'll never totally understand them."

That night, Lou sat in bed watching Judy undress and put on her nightgown. Smiling Judy climbed into bed beside Lou. "The kids told me you had quite a brouhaha this afternoon. How's your booboo?"

"It needs some kisses."

Judy reached across the bed and turned off the light, then snuggled down beside her husband.

Chapter 13

Earlier that evening, Betty had gotten ready for the prom with little time to spare. Jimmy came by at five o'clock to pick her up. They were first going back to his house so his dad could take movies of them with his 8mm camera. Betty had never been in a movie before and was really excited about it.

Jimmy had reservations at an upscale expensive restaurant for supper at six o'clock. After the prom several couples were going to meet at Lucy Monroe's house for a swimming party and an early breakfast. The Monroes lived in a large house with an in-the-ground pool. Lucy was their only child. Betty tried not to envy Lucy, but she couldn't help it. Betty did not know that Lucy envied Betty with a sister so close for companionship.

The picture taking went well. Betty was wearing a strapless mint green lace dress of which Lou did not approve. Judy refused to buy Betty the shoes with very high heels she had chosen. Betty paid for them herself. She had the shoe maker dye them green to match her dress.

At the restaurant, Betty was not given a menu. She wasn't sure what to do. The waiter asked Jimmy what she wanted. This was displeasing to her. Why couldn't she pick her own meal? Jimmy ordered lobster tails. Betty ate only a small amount. She was so excited about the prom her stomach was in a knot. Eating the butter dipped fish caused her to have an upset stomach. She had also read in some magazine that they were very high in calories. Jimmy ate all of his and finished eating her meal.

They arrived at the gym just as the band began to play. The gym had been turned into a fairyland. It was almost unrecognizable as a gym. There was a large glass ball hanging from the ceiling. A light reflected from it as it turned. Under the glass ball was what appeared to be a tropical island. All the side walls were decorated with green leaves and flowers attached to brown paper vines to look like hanging gardens. Betty wondered, "How did they ever do it?" She knew next year, as a junior, her class would be responsible for the prom. She decided she wasn't going to have any part of decorating. Maybe she would volunteer to help with refreshments. The small cakes called petit fours didn't look so daunting.

Jimmy was a good dancer. Betty felt like a klutz. Her parents didn't approve of dancing and she hadn't been to many dances. A couple of her friends had tried to show her some dance steps which she hadn't mastered. Her very high heeled shoes didn't help either. Finally, Jimmy asked if she would mind if he danced with other girls? What could she say but, "No, I don't mind. Go ahead." For most of the evening she sat and watched as he danced first with one girl and then another.

The prom ended at eleven-thirty. Jimmy drove in a different direction than toward the Monroe house. "Where are you going Jimmy? The party is in the other direction."

"A bunch of guys and their dates are

meeting at the ice cream parlor in Wellington. It's really a nice place. Have you ever been there?"

"Yes, with my family. It does serve good ice cream, still I'm not really hungry."

"You don't go there just to eat. It's a super hang out. Did you have a good time tonight? I'm sorry about you not wanting to dance more."

"Oh, I had a wonderful time. I enjoyed watching you. You're really a good dancer."

Betty recognized several cars in the parking lot. There was music coming from the parlor's open door. Jimmy and Betty walked in. A number of couples were dancing. Some of the boys snickered and punched one another. She thought, "What's going on?"

Jimmy ordered each of them a chocolate

malt. Betty was not particularly fond of malts and drank only a small amount. She pushed it towards Jimmy and asked if he wanted to finish it. He did. Jimmy asked her to dance. She did, stepping on his shoes a couple of times and stumbling. They sat down. She encouraged him to ask some other girl to dance. She said she was okay just watching.

They left the parlor an hour later. Betty was getting tired. She had planned to take a nap during the day. Because of having helped Mavis she didn't have a chance. Maybe she would have an opportunity to catch a quick nap at the Monroes.

Jimmy seemed to be driving endlessly. She was having a hard time staying awake and wasn't sure where they were. Finally, she realized they were driving down a dirt road leading to the old gravel pit. In the day-time, during the warm weather months, people went swimming in the pit and picnicked in the surrounding woods. At night, it was notorious as a teen lovers' lane.

"Jimmy, turn the car around. I know where we're headed and I don't want to go there."

"Come on Betty. I've put out a lot of money to show you a good time. Now it's your turn to put out for me."

Judy had talked to her older girls about the "facts of life". Judy was expecting another baby and Betty knew why. "Stop the car and turn it around! I don't plan on having a baby just a few months younger than my sibling."

'Sibling' was a word Jimmy had never heard before and wasn't sure what Betty meant. "Relax Betty, all I want to do is have a little fun."

"I know what kind of 'fun' you want to have. Take me home."

Jimmy stopped the car, "Let's go for a walk."

"In these heels?"

"Take them off."

"And walk in my nylons?"

"You can take them off too."

"Then what next, my underpants?"

Jimmy gave a nervous laugh and reached for Betty, "Come on, loosen up."

Betty smacked his hand and opened the car door. She started to get out and Jimmy grabbed her dress, tearing the lace. Her left heel got caught in the door frame causing her to fall to the ground. Jimmy opened his door and started around to her side. Betty jumped up, removed her other heel, gathered up her dress and headed back down the road as fast as she could in stocking feet while holding up her dress.

Jimmy got back into the car, turned it around and headed after her. She managed to reach the blacktop road before Jimmy caught up to her. He pulled up beside her and turned down the passenger window. "Get in the car Betty."

"No!"

"You can't walk all the way home."

"Do you see that house down the road? It's the Ogdon's house. I'm going to go there, wake them up and call my dad."

"No Betty, please don't. I'm sorry, I'll take you home." Betty ignored him and continued walking. Jimmy drove along beside her, pleading with her to get into the car.

All at once another car drove up behind them and suddenly the night was lit up with flashing red lights. Jimmy groaned. Betty turned around just as Sean got out of the squad car. She ran to the car, breathing deeply and placed her hands on the hood of the squad as Sean walked up to her. "Oh Sean, am I glad to see you!"

"What's going on Betty? Who's in the car?"

"It's Jimmy Palmer. He took me to the prom. We had a really good time and were supposed to go to Lucy Monroe's house for a swim party afterward. Instead, Jimmy drove to the gravel pit. I told him to take me home; he wouldn't, so I got out of the car and started to walk."

"Did he hurt you?"

"No, nothing happened, well, I lost a shoe getting out of the car and Jimmy grabbed ahold of my dress and tore it. I took off my other shoe so I could walk, and now my nylons are ruined." As hard as she tried not to, Betty began to cry. She didn't want to seem weak. "We had such a good time and now he's ruined it."

Sean came to Betty's side and put his arm around her leading her to the passenger side of his car. He reached into the back for a blanket to put around her shoulders. "Sit in the car while I talk to Jimmy."

Sean walked to the driver's side of Jimmy's car. He leaned in and lit up Jimmy's face with his flashlight. "What's going on Jimmy?"

Jimmy bent his head down while both

hands gripped the steering wheel. He looked up into the light at Sean, "Nothing."

"Nothing? Why is Betty's dress torn? Why was she walking in stocking feet? And why is she crying right now in my cruiser? That doesn't seem like nothing to me."

"I tried to get her to go to the gravel pit. You know how it is. I spent a lot of money on her. She should be willing to give a little."

"That's not how it is Jimmy. I'll tell you what." Sean got out his notebook and a pen. "You make an itemized list of your expenses and we'll take it to Betty's father. I'm sure Mr. Hunt will be happy to reimburse you for all the money you put out for tonight."

Jimmy only eyeballed the notebook. "You don't understand. Some of the guys at school dared me to take Betty to the pit. They said they were all going to go there."

"I do understand Jimmy. You're acting like a jerk. A real man stands up for himself and does what is right. He doesn't let others make decisions for him. How old are you?"

"I'll be eighteen in a couple of weeks."

Sean sighed deeply, "That's lucky for you. You're really fortunate, it's not a couple of weeks ago, that you turned eighteen. If you were already eighteen, you could be in a heap of trouble. You could be charged with attempted rape." Sean thought Jimmy was going to faint when he heard him say that. "As it is, I'm going to follow you to the Hunt house. You can tell Mr. and Mrs. Hunt how you behaved tonight with their daughter."

"No, please. Just let me apologize to Betty. I'm really sorry."

"When you get to the intersection, make a right. Their house is a half mile down. We'll be right behind you."

Betty went into the house using the dining room door followed by Sean and a very frightened Jimmy. She climbed the stairs more tired than she could ever remember being before in her life. Her parents' door was open. "Mom, Dad, please get up. Sean O'Toole is here. He wants to talk to you."

Lou was at the door before Betty finished. He saw how she looked, "Have you been in an accident? What's happened?"

"Just come downstairs, please." Betty turned and retraced her weary steps back to the dining room. She sat down in a chair placing her elbows on the table and cupping her head between her hands.

Lou was right behind her. He saw Sean and Jimmy standing on the other side of the table. "What's wrong Sean? Jimmy, did you hurt Betty?" As he said this he started ominously towards Jimmy.

Sean raised his hand toward Lou, "Hold on Lou, Betty's not hurt."

Judy entered the room and drew up a chair by Betty and sat down. She put her arms around her daughter. Betty rested her head on Judy's shoulder.

Sean continued, "Betty, are you up to telling your mom and dad what happened tonight?"

Betty lifted her head off her mother's shoulder and nodded. Drained of emotion she repeated the events of the evening.

As she finished, Lou once again advanced toward Jimmy, "You good-for-nothing! You ought to be horse whipped! I let you take my daughter out, believing you're an alright guy and this is how you treat her?"

At last, Jimmy answered meekly, "I'm sorry Mr. Hunt. I know what I did was wrong. I've never done anything like this before."

Lou again advanced towards Jimmy. "So why did you think you could practice on my daughter?"

Sean put up his hands to stop Lou. "Calm down Lou."

Jimmy went on with his reasoning for what happened, "It's just that all the guys said that they were going to take their dates to the gravel pit."

"So next year, if you're in the Army and a bunch of guys come up to you saying they're going to swipe some equipment to sell on the black market, are you going to go along with them? Or, if you're in college and go to a party and a table is full of pills and your friends say, 'grab a handful, we're all using it'. Are you going to be a lemming and go over the cliff with them? You'd better grow a backbone. Be a man and do what's right!" Lou was almost shouting by now.

"Yes sir. I hear you."

"You'd better, because I don't ever want you near Betty again. Don't even talk to her. And I'd better not hear of anyone at school talking about this. If they do, I'll know it came from you and I'll press charges. Do you understand?"

"Yes sir."

Sean finally intervened, "Lou, Mrs. Hunt,

is there anything more you need to know from Jimmy?" Both parents shook their heads. "Then I'm going to follow Jimmy home and have a talk with his parents. Let's go Jimmy."

After they left, Judy asked Betty if she would like help getting to bed. No one had noticed Darlene standing in the shadows. "Let me help her Mom. You and dad go back to bed. I'll stay down here with her." She went to Betty and helped her out of the chair. "Come on Sis, I'll help you out of your clothes and rub some lotion on your feet."

Betty looked down at her spoilt dress and commented as the two sisters walked to her bedroom, "Look at my beautiful dress, it's ruined."

"It's okay, I figured the first prom I went to I'd have to wear it. Now I'll get a new one!"

Darlene turned to her folks, "Mom and Dad, you can sleep in tomorrow. I'll get up with the kids and keep them quiet." Her parents stared at her in amazement.

Chapter 14

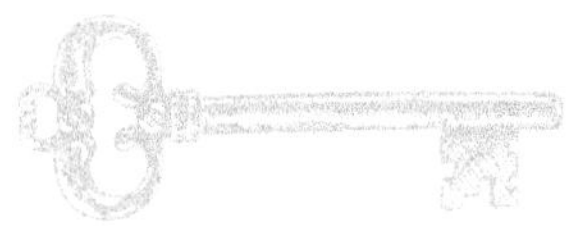

Sunday morning Lou came down the stairs about eight o'clock. He could smell coffee. Entering the kitchen, he saw his three youngest sitting around the kitchen table eating bowls of cereal. In front of each was an uneaten plate of scrambled eggs. "Good morning, Daddy. Darlene is cooking this morning," voiced Gloria.

"I can see that. What's wrong? You're not eating the eggs."

Before the other children had a chance to say anything, Darlene answered him, "I didn't do a very good job cooking them.

They're sort of rubbery. Would you like a cup of coffee?"

"Yes, thank you." Trying to soothe Darlene's ego he added, "Eggs can be difficult to get just right." Darlene set a cup of coffee down in front of him. Lou took a swallow and almost gagged. It was the worst coffee he had ever tasted. It was even worse than any he had drunk before going on mid-watch in the Navy. "Louis, pass me the milk jug and the sugar. Thanks."

"I thought you always drank your coffee black."

"Yes Louis, I usually do. This morning I decided I needed a little extra something in it."

Lou decided to take the three younger children to Sunday School and not stay for church. He asked Darlene to get the girls ready while he and Louis cleaned up the kitchen. Louis objected stating it was "women's work".

Lou informed him that when he got married, his wife would expect him to know how to do dishes, so he might as well start learning now. Before going upstairs to get ready himself, Lou dumped out the coffee and made a fresh pot.

That afternoon Judy was sitting on the porch drinking coffee. On the floor near her, Gloria was sleeping on a blanket and Connie was working a puzzle. Out in the front yard, Louis and Lou were playing ball. Betty was reading a book sitting at the dining room table, and Darlene was actually sitting at the table doing homework. A white Buick sedan turned into the driveway. Judy didn't recognize it at first, until she saw Ron and Mary Palmer in the front seat. Jimmy was slouched down in the back seat. She sighed. She really didn't want to see them, "Lou?"

"Yeah, I see them. Louis go in the house and watch TV or something. I think the Tigers are playing the White Sox today."

The car stopped and Ron and Mary got out. Ron took a couple of steps toward the house then turned and motioned for Jimmy to get out. Jimmy reluctantly opened the door and walked behind his father. Lou went over to Ron. Mary Palmer continued walking up to the porch. Judy got up and went to the edge of the porch. Mary stopped at the steps.

"Hello Judy. Ron and I thought we should come by to talk about last night. We are so sorry and embarrassed our son acted the way he did."

"That's kind of you Mary. Come on up to the table and sit down. Would you like a cup of coffee?"

"No thank you. We won't stay long. I really don't know what to say. I'm humiliated and ashamed."

"Mary, parents teach their children the best they know how. When they're little it's easier to see they behave right. When they get older, no matter what they've been taught, they make their own choices. Look at Adam and Eve. They had the perfect parent. Think how God must have felt when they chose to do what He had told them not to."

Mary replied with a heavy sigh, "You're right Judy. Thank you for the kind words. Hopefully, Jimmy has learned a lesson he won't forget."

"My grandfather often said, 'You just hope you can keep your kids from getting into serious trouble before they get over fool's hill'." Judy smiled sincerely at Mary as she said this. Her heart ached for the woman.

In the yard, the two men and Jimmy were having their own discussion. "Lou, when O'Toole brought Jimmy home last night, I was seeing red. I felt like beating the tar out of him. I'm just thankful Betty had more sense than he did and nothing more happened. I thought I had brought him up better than that. We had a long talk last night and into the morning. He's grounded for the summer and can only use his car to go to work and back. I don't think he'll do anything like that again. Jimmy, don't you have something to say to Mr. Hunt?"

Jimmy stood with his head down, kicking dirt around with one foot. He lifted his head and looked Lou in the eye. "Mr. Hunt, I want to apologize again for last night. I was stupid. If you'll tell me how much Betty's dress, shoes and ah, nylons cost, I'll pay for them. If you'd let me, I'd also like to apologize to Betty. I promise not to say anything at school."

Lou stood looking at Jimmy for several seconds. He was still angry, but he knew he should accept what Jimmy said at face value. "I accept your apology, and I will send you a bill for the damages. I don't know if Betty wants to see you. Just a minute." Lou left the father and son standing in the yard and went into the house. Betty was watching from a dining room window. Lou asked, "Do you want to see Jimmy? He just apologized to me again." She said she would.

Outside she stood on the porch. Jimmy

came closer, stopping at the bottom of the steps. "Betty, I was a real jerk last night. I could just kick myself for being so stupid. I'm really sorry. Please forgive me. I promise not to say anything at school about what happened."

Betty thought he seemed sincere. She was still angry and hurt. As a Christian she knew, she had to forgive Jimmy, "I accept your apology. I still don't ever want to see you again." She turned and went back into the house and started crying.

Darlene looked up from her studying. She went over to Betty. "Why are you crying?"

"I feel like I did something wrong. Like it was my fault for what happened last night."

"Betty, that's just the devil making you feel that way. It wasn't your fault. You did nothing wrong. Just say, 'Satan leave me alone.'"

Betty looked up at Darlene, "What about tomorrow at school? I know my friends are going to ask me about the prom, what do I say?"

"Tell them the truth. Say the gym was decorated beautifully and you had a wonderful time. Tell them Lucy Monroe invited some couples to her house for a swim, but you were so tired you asked Jimmy to bring you home. None of that is a lie."

"What if someone says they've heard gossip about what else happened?"

"Do like you do to me. Look at them with your blank stare and walk away."

Betty looked at Darlene, smiled, then laughed.

Monday had come and gone with no one at school asking Betty any embarrassing questions. Tuesday, Mr. Weitendorf, the Auto Mechanics' teacher came up to Betty, "I overheard a couple of the boys talking to Jimmy Palmer." Betty's heart plunged into her stomach. "From what I could gather the boys had dared Jimmy to take you to the gravel pit after the prom. Jimmy told them you were too nice a girl to do that to. You can be proud to have such a good reputation. Don't ever do anything that will cause it to be tarnished."

Betty didn't know how to respond. All she could think of to say was, "Thank you". She went to her next class with a lightness in her heart. She felt clean inside.

Late that afternoon, Len Rheimes, the only remaining thief from the beer garden robbery, sat, on a tree stump near the gravel pit, sulking. He was hungry. He thought about going to ask for help from his oldest sister, 'Goodie Two Shoes' Leah. He quickly shrugged the thought off. Leah would call the sheriff as soon as she laid eyes on him. Len's other sister, Karen, was closer in age to him. As children they often played together and got along fairly well. Karen had already helped him, a couple of weeks ago, with some food and a few dollars. She had told him not to come back. Her husband would be furious if he found out what she had done. Karen was afraid of what he might do to her.

Chapter 15

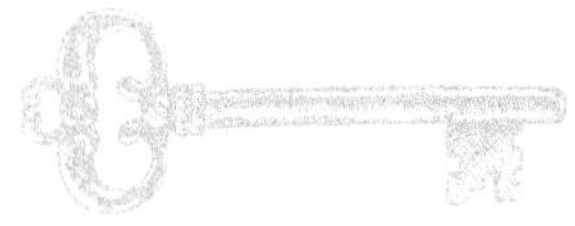

True to her word, Monday morning Mavis walked over to the sheriff's department. Sean O'Toole sat talking to Thelma while sitting on the edge of her desk. He stood as Mavis entered, "Hello Mavis, what a pleasant surprise! What can we do for you?" He pulled out a chair, "Sit down. Can I get you a cup of coffee?"

"No thank you, I've already had two cups this morning. I have some information about a relative of mine who disappeared in 1932."

"Ah, and you're wondering if it could be the Hunts' skeleton. Tell me about it."

Mavis repeated her story about Uncle Irving. Sean tried to take notes. However, he was having a problem concentrating on what Mavis was saying. He was more interested in watching her.

Mavis finished and there was silence in the room. Sean just gawked at Mavis. Thelma cleared her throat. "Sean, do you have any questions for Mavis?" Sean shook his head. "Well, I've been taking some notes. Mavis, let me repeat what I wrote, to be sure it's correct." Mavis nodded as Thelma read her notes.

When Mavis left, Thelma gave her notes to Sean. "Here Lover Boy, when the sheriff returns maybe you should share these with him."

"Thanks, Thelma."

Sheriff Dave Byrne returned about an hour later. He and Sean sat in his office as Sean read Thelma's notes. "I was just a kid in 1932, but I seem to remember something about a disappearance. Are you leaving to go on patrol?" Sean nodded. "I'll let you know what we find."

"THELMA!" Thelma stuck her head into the sheriff's office. "Go downstairs and find the case report on Irving Steel."

The basement was where old records were kept. They dated back to 1870. The records were in good order. One of the first jobs Thelma had been given, seven years ago, when she was hired, was to, "Straighten out the record files in the basement". It had taken her almost a month. She was sure when an officer was finished with a record, he simply tossed it down the steps.

She knew that was really not true, still the area had been an absolute mess. From then on, she required all files and records to be placed in the designated "in box" on her desk for her to file. When a file was needed, she was the one to retrieve it. Only if she wasn't working, which wasn't often, only then, could someone else go to the basement to collect a file. Fortunately, Sheriff Byrne backed her in the process. Thelma had no trouble locating the record the sheriff was after. She sat down on a stool and skimmed through the record. It was basically the same information Mavis had related.

"Sheriff, here's what you asked for."

Dave looked through it. "Hmm, this man was six feet two inches. It says he also broke his right collar bone as a kid. Here is the number of the Michigan State Lab that has the bones from the Hunt's attic. Give them a call. Tell them we are trying to locate an Irving Steel that went missing about 1932. We know that he was over six feet tall and broke his collar bone as a kid. Ask if they think the skeleton was that tall and if he or she ever had a broken collar bone."

It took two days and several phone calls until finally Thelma was able to talk to a technician who knew about the skeleton. The technician wouldn't tell Thelma anything on the telephone. He promised to let her know as soon as he could. Four days later just after lunch, a young man dressed in a black suit and gray tie walked into the office. Thelma thought he looked about her brother's age of nineteen. He showed Thelma a badge and identification card. He was from the FBI. She decided he must be older than he looked. He asked to see Sheriff Byrne.

Thelma showed the agent into the sheriff's office. The agent shut the door. After nearly an hour both Dave Byrne and the agent came out, "Thelma, I'm taking Special Agent Reeves to see Mavis."

Dave had called Mavis before leaving his office so she was expecting them. She was finishing her last customer of the day when the two men entered her salon. "I'll be with you in just a jiffy. Go upstairs and have a seat in the living room. I promise not to be long."

The men were sitting uncomfortably in overstuffed chairs when Mavis came into the room. "I'm sorry to intrude on your work Mavis. This is Special Agent John Reeves of the FBI. He wants to talk to you about Irving Steel."

"Good afternoon, Miss Hampton. I'm sorry to interrupt your work."

"It's no problem. The lady I just finished was my last customer for the day. I'm sure by now it's all over town about Sheriff Byrne and a strange man coming to see me." Mavis smiled as she said this. "Is the skeleton my uncle?"

"No, it isn't. Your uncle was over six feet tall. As I understand it, whoever the skeleton was, was no more than five feet seven or eight inches. Also, it never had a broken collar bone. I will tell you what we know about your uncle. Your aunt never told you anything?"

"No, she said the FBI never gave her any information."

"She probably didn't want you to know anything bad about him. According to our records she was contacted in 1933 with the information we had."

"Oh, what information? I'd like to know."

He dug into the vest pocket of his suit and unfolded a piece of paper, "Irving Steel was a small-time bootlegger. During prohibition he drove to Port Huron, where he had a partner, Leroy Muller, who owned an auto ferry. This was used to cross over into and out of Canada."

"Why didn't they use the Blue Water Bridge?"

"If I remember right, it wasn't built until 1938. Anyway, your uncle was so ingenious at hiding the whiskey he smuggled into the U. S., he wasn't even on the FBI's suspect list. Most of the illegal alcohol coming into the U. S. came through Windsor into Detroit.

"Your uncle and Leroy made the mistake of moving their operation from Port Huron to Detroit when the Detroit to Windsor tunnel was opened in 1930. They continued their smuggling operation until his disappearance in 1932. The FBI learned, after he disappeared, that he was so good, the Detroit Purple Gang sought to enlist him into their organization. They controlled the bootlegging from Canada. Your uncle probably refused their offer, and we believe The Purple Gang had him killed. His partner was wiser and joined the gang. Even Al Capone feared the Purple Gang and made a partnership with them."

"Was my uncle's body ever found?"

"A very badly decomposed body was found just outside of Grosse Point Park. Your aunt was asked to look at it. She thought

it might be her husband but wouldn't
say for sure.

"We know she received money every
month anonymously. This probably came
from your uncle's partner, Leroy, because it
stopped about the time he died in 1946."

Chapter 16

In late May, Harriet Seymour, Judy's mother accepted an invitation to visit. It depressed Judy to think she had to invite her mother to visit. She could go to her in-laws anytime and wasn't surprised when, on any given day, they might show up at her home. Her own mother wouldn't come unless invited.

One reason for this necessity was because Harriet belonged to a number of civic organizations. She was usually scheduled for a garden club meeting, a hospital auxiliary meeting or a meeting for anyone of her many other interests. Judy thought her mother should give Darlene lessons in organization.

Harriet arrived promptly at 1:30 as scheduled. Before getting out of her car, she put the top up on her 1965, red Cadillac convertible, then closed the windows. Judy stood in the dining room watching her mother walk to the house. Her slenderness made her appear taller than her five feet five inches. She wore a bright blue linen summer suit with blue heeled shoes. Her dark auburn hair was done in the latest Jackie Kennedy flipped-bob style. Mrs. Kennedy was still hugely popular even though she had not been seen in public much since the assassination of her husband in 1963. Judy opened the dining room door. "Hi Mom, it's so nice to see you. Wouldn't you like to sit out here on the porch?"

"For goodness sakes no! Every time a car goes down the road a cloud of dust follows. My suit would be brown."

Judy defensively answered her mother, "That's not true Mother, the township oils the road in front of the house to keep down the dust."

"Well, it doesn't stop the dust from flying on either side of the oil, now does it! You notice that I put the top up on my car. I have no intention of sitting on a dust covered seat."

"This isn't getting off to a good start", thought Judy. Aloud she said to her mother, "Okay, let's sit here in the dining room. There's a nice cross breeze. Would you like some lemonade? I just made it."

"Did you use real lemons?"

Judy sighed, "No, it's a lemonade mix."

"No thank you. I'll just have a glass of your well water." Harriet had no sooner sat down when she asked, "So why did you want me to come? I hope it's not to tell me you're pregnant again."

Judy had returned from the kitchen with two glasses, one held water, the other lemonade. "That's not the reason I asked you here."

"Well thank goodness for that."

"However, as it happens, I am expecting again."

"Really Judith! I would think you would be embarrassed. " Both women sat staring at each other. "So, when is the blessed event to occur?"

"My due date is November tenth."

"You're going to be miserable all through the summer."

"That's not necessarily true."

"Well, you were born in September, and I was miserable!"

As long as Judy could remember she had been told what an arduous time her mother had during her pregnancy. Harriet had claimed Judy had a "big" head and decided to never get pregnant again.

"Really mother, sometimes I just don't understand you. Anyway, do you remember Alice Higgins? She was Mike Hunt's fiancée. The last time anyone ever saw her was at Mike's funeral. Didn't she work at the hospital when you were there?"

"Do I remember her? You bet I do. I hope she lost her nursing license. "

"Why's that?"

"I was working the three to eleven-thirty shift. Alice was scheduled for the eleven to seven-thirty shift. She never showed up. Of course, I had to stay until the night supervisor could get a replacement. You know, a nurse cannot abandon her patients. It happened to be a time when your father was out of town on a business trip. Your grandmother Webber was caring for you. She was very upset when I phoned to tell her. Finally, at about three a.m. one of the day nurses came in early to relieve me."

Judy asked, "Did you ever find out why Alice didn't come to work?"

"No. And as far as I know, no one ever did. Wait just a minute! Are you thinking the skeleton in your attic might be Alice?"

"Oh, I hope not. I really can't think how she would have come to be up there with a rope around her neck."

Harriet explained, "Alice was really distraught after Mike died. She was hoping Mike's dad would let them live out here after they got married. She was always going on about how nice this place was. I sure can't see why."

"Well, thank you Mother. This does happen to be a nice place, especially to raise children."

"Sorry Judith. I'm wondering about what might have happened. What if she came out here alone, to mourn, the day of the funeral? Some fellow saw her and tried to get friendly with her. She resisted and he killed her, most likely by accident."

"I hope that's not the case. I feel so badly

when I think about some woman lying in the attic unmourned. And no one knowing about her for all these years. What do you remember about Alice?"

"Hmmm, Alice inherited her aunt's house. It was so big she took in a couple of women boarders. Maybe one of them knows what happened to her."

"Can you recall their names?"

"Oh, let me think. One was a teacher. She taught in a two-room school in Drayton Park. She taught the lower grades, first through fourth. I remember Alice gave her some things to use for a lesson on health. Oh darn, what was her name?"

"What about Alice's other boarder? Can you recall her name?"

"Iva Doig."

"You mean of the Doig family that had the terrible fire?"

"Yes, it was her family. What an awful thing it was! I wasn't sure you would remember it. You were only about ten."

"One of the girls who died was in my class. I remember her because she sat right in front of me. Afterward the teacher left the seat empty for the rest of the year."

"Oh, it was terrible. Just terrible! The injured were brought to the hospital. I was called down to help out in E. R. The Doig baby was still alive. He was burned so horribly we transferred him to Hurley Hospital in Flint. I think he died a few days later."

"Iva was the oldest girl. Her older brother had burns on his face and arms. I don't remember his name. He had gone into the house trying to get the other children out. He was only able to rescue the baby. The father showed up at the hospital so drunk, he didn't even know what was happening.

"After the fire, Norm Makenzie gave Iva a job in his drug store. The boy joined the Army."

"I wish we could talk to her or Alice's other boarder."

"Eleanor Hanover."

"What?"

"Eleanor Hanover is the name of the other boarder. I wonder if she's still teaching in Drayton Park? Would you like me to check if she is?"

"You would do that?"

"I would. It would be interesting. Kind of like a detective!"

"There is one thing you should know."

Harriet looked at her daughter suspiciously, "What is it?"

"Walt and Joan are also doing some nosing around. As a matter-of-fact, Walt got into trouble with Sean O'Toole. He was questioning Richard Thornton about his brother Joel and Jennifer Mitcham, who both went missing back in 1918."

"I remember them. I went to school with Jennifer. As for Sean, I used to babysit him. I've changed his diapers. He doesn't scare me." Mother and daughter finally laughed together as the tension ebbed.

"You do know, don't you, your father and Norm Makenzie are good friends? They went to the same college. It was your father who convinced Norm to open the drug store here after he graduated from pharmacy school. You should ask your father if he would talk to Norm about Iva."

"Thanks Mom. I know you're busy so I'll give Dad a call."

"Oh my! Look at the time. I have a meeting with the hospital auxiliary at three. Must run! I'll let you know what I find out about Eleanor Hanover."

Judy watched her mother's car go up the lane. She could never remember being called anything except Judith by her mother. There had never been an endearing expression; never, Honey, Sweetheart or Darling. Nor could she recall ever receiving a hug from Harriet. That was why her mother's offer to help, surprised Judy. Harriet was usually busy with her clubs, organizations and auxiliaries.

That night Judy's father unexpectedly

called her. "Hi Judy, your mother told me about the visit the two of you had this afternoon. It sounds interesting. I'd like to help. Want me to ask Norm about Iva? I remember her, a pretty girl, bright too."

"I didn't know you knew her."

"I guess you don't remember. I was on the volunteer fire department when the Doig place burned down. It was a terrible fire. I think the worst I've ever been to. Some of the volunteer fireman quit after working the fire.

"The place was so old, once the fire took hold, it went up like a matchbox. When we arrived with one of the tankers, Max, the oldest boy, came staggering out the front door carrying a baby. Iva and two younger sisters were sitting on the ground coughing and choking. The father was lying in some weeds a short distance away drunk as a skunk. Max handed me the baby and said, his mother, a sister and a brother were still in the house. Then he collapsed. The whole house crumbled into a ball of fire. There was nothing we could do."

Judy could hear sorrow in his voice, "Oh Dad, it sounds horrible."

"It was. Max and the baby were taken to Hurley Hospital in Flint. The baby died three days later. Max had burns on his face and arms. He was months recovering."

"Was it ever determined how the fire started?"

"It's believed a tea kettle was left on a lit burner. The water boiled away and the metal actually melted down the side of the stove. There were rags or something on the floor by the stove that caught fire."

"What ever happened to the younger sisters?"

Martin was quiet for several seconds before replying, "I guess it's okay to tell you. I asked your mother to allow the two younger girls to come live with us. I thought they would be good companions for you. She would not agree. An older couple in Wellington, Mr. and Mrs. Ferguson, took them in. They had no children of their own and were good parents to the girls. The Fergusons are both gone now. But before Mr. Ferguson passed, I saw him getting gas one day. I asked about the girls, he said both girls married well, one lives in England and the other in California. I don't have either of the girls' addresses."

"Do you know where Max lives? Would he know how to reach Iva?"

"Max was only seventeen at the time. His father signed for him to enlist. He died on D-Day."

"What a sad story! Do you think Mr. Makenzie would remember Iva?"

"I don't know. I plan on visiting him next week and I'll ask about her. Do you think Walt and Gully would like to go with me? Norm lives alone and loves company."

"I'm sure they would. Give Walt a call."

"I will, Sweetheart. I love you. Bye"

"I love you too Dad. Good bye." Judy felt warm all over as she hung up the receiver.

The next day Harriet telephoned the Drayton Park Grade School, "Good morning, this is Mrs. Harriet Seymour. I'm trying to locate Eleanor Hanover. She taught at the two-room school in 1942, before the present grade school was built. Does she still teach there?"

"No, there is no teacher here by that name."

"Is there someone who might remember her?"

"Miss Perry, our principal taught in one of the old schools before consolidation. Maybe she remembers your friend. I'll put you on hold and ask her."

Harriet waited impatiently for what seemed like a very long time. She didn't like being "put on hold". Eventually a sweet soft voice came on the line. "Hello, this is Miss Perry. My secretary said you are asking about Eleanor. May I inquire why?"

Just as sweetly, Harriet replied, "Thank you Miss Perry, for taking my call." Harriet was experienced in getting people to cooperate. "Eleanor was a boarder in the home of an acquaintance of mine in 1942. It is this other woman I'm actually trying to locate. I've lost her address." Harriet considered this was near enough to the truth not to be a lie. Miss Perry did not respond. Harriet at first wondered if the connection had been lost.

At last Miss Perry stated, "Eleanor left here in 1947. She married a young veteran and they moved to Detroit. I still correspond with her. If you will give me your address and telephone number, I'll write Eleanor, and she can decide if she wishes to contact you."

Harriet was a bit miffed and was about to argue but decided Miss Perry might refuse to do even that much. "Thank you. Miss Perry, I truly appreciate your taking your valuable time to assist me."

"It is quite all right. I'll get the letter off

tomorrow." After getting Harriet's address and telephone number, she said good-bye and hung up.

Harriet hung up and immediately wrote Miss Perry a thank you note. She was, if nothing else, very proper.

Chapter 17

Martin Seymour, Judy's father, thought about his promise to visit his friend, the old druggist, Norm Makenzie. Norm's wife, Julia had passed away several years ago. Norm was a lonely man with one daughter who lived in Traverse City, several hundred miles away. Martin tried to visit Norm a couple of times a month although his guilt told him he should visit more often. When he did go to see Norm, he had Flora, the maid, prepare a food basket. Norm was no longer able to drive and was dependent on people bringing him the things he needed.

Martin called Walt and asked him if he and Gully wanted to go with him; after all it was their investigation. They could stay for lunch and give Norm a good visit. Walt and Gully were happy to go with Martin.

Two days later, Gully drove to Walt's house and Martin picked up both men there. Martin had advised them they should plan on staying most of the day. Norm was lonely and liked to talk. This didn't seem to bother either man.

Their destination was just outside of the village limits on five acres. The once manicured lawn was now full of weeds. A young man was hired to mow and did nothing else. The attractive gardens, Norm and his deceased wife, had spent so much time cultivating, were no more. The hired lawn mower simply mowed everything. Untrimmed shrubbery covered the front windows.

 "What a sorrowful sight! Can't something be done about this mess?" asked Gully.

"Norm's daughter is trying to get him to move to a care facility near her. She doesn't want anything done to the house, hoping he will see the absurdity of staying here."

"You're talking about a nursing home, aren't you"?voiced Walt.

"Well, yes that's right that's the next step. He really shouldn't be living by himself. He can't drive anymore and he even has a difficult time walking. The thing is, he's still very alert mentally."

The car made its way up the rutted drive. Norm was sitting on the front porch rocking, watching for his visitors. He got up sluggishly and waited on the porch, grinning from ear to ear. The three men got out of the car and walked up to the porch each carrying a box. The porch rails were covered in twining vines that continued across a good part of the floor.

"Hi Martin, so good to see you. Well hello Walt! I haven't seen you in more than a month-of-Sundays. How's that pretty wife of yours and those grandkids? They must be getting quite big. How many do you have now? Who's this with you? I think I've seen you around town a time or two."

"Hold on Norm. You're going to talk yourself silly before we have a chance to answer any of your questions."

"Sorry Martin, it's just that I miss people so."

With a twinkle in his eye, Walt said, "Yes,

you really liked to keep people talking in your store. I always thought you figured the longer they stayed, the more they'd buy."

This evoked a chuckle from Norm, "You're right Walt. You're surely right."

Gully offered his hand to Norm and said, "My name's Henry Gullington. Most folks call me Gully."

"You're that retired soldier. I've heard a lot about you. Quite a hero!"

"Thanks. I only did what was expected of any soldier."

"Let's get out of this sun. We can go in the backyard if we want to stay outside. It's in the shade."

The men entered a sparsely furnished living room. Martin stopped with an astonished look on his face, "What's happened to all your furniture?"

"It's that daughter of mine. Every time she comes, which isn't often, she takes something. She was here last week and took my wife's desk and chair. The girl said since I do all my writing and bill paying at the kitchen table, I don't need the desk anymore. She doesn't understand how it comforted me to look at the desk and picture my Julia sitting there writing letters."

"I'm sorry Norm." Martin felt uncomfortable and changed the subject. "Flora made up some goodies for you. Let me put them in the Frigidaire®. She also packed us a lunch." Martin walked into the kitchen. The table was covered with newspapers, magazines and mail. "Let's go in the backyard like you suggested."

"First I'll make coffee."

"There's no need. I have two thermoses with coffee."

The four men walked through the kitchen to the backyard and sat in the shade around a picnic table. They bantered around for some time. At length, Martin said, "Norm, do you remember Iva Doig?"

"Sure, I do. She was about the best worker I ever had."

"Do you know what happened to her? It seems she was working one day and the next she was gone."

"That's exactly what happened. Why are you asking about her?"

Martin hesitated not sure how to respond. He was relieved when Walt answered instead, "A couple of months ago, my grandkids discovered the skeleton of a woman in their attic. You probably remember, they live in the old Hunt farmhouse."

"And you think it might be Iva?"

"We're just trying to account for all the women who have gone missing in the past twenty-five years or so."

Norm began to laugh, "That's a good one. I can't wait to tell Iva."

Gully piped up, "Then you know where she is?"

"Sure I do. She lives in Detroit. She's married and has three kids."

"Tell us what happened that caused her to disappear so suddenly," stated Walt.

"She came to work for me after that terrible fire that killed her mother and those kids. She was really a good worker. The problem was her old man. He was a terrible drunk. He'd come to the store two, three times a week asking Iva for money. She'd give him what she could. She really needed the money for herself to live on. I resented him taking what little she had. I told her, I wasn't paying her to keep her dad in booze.

"She was such a shy, timid thing. Her pa was just no good. I shooed him out of the building many times. Then I was in a terrible auto accident. You remember it, don't you Martin?" Martin nodded.

Norm looked at Gully and continued. "I couldn't work for several months, about six if I remember right. Anyway, what do you do when it's a one-man pharmacy? I hired a young pharmacist just out of college. He was a fine-looking man; he knew it and was very conceited. Besides that, he was 4-F for some reason or another." Norm said this with bitterness in his voice. Many people still resented those men who hadn't served in the war, even if they had been classified as unfit for military service.

"I didn't care for him. Actually, I had no choice. The war was on, and most of the pharmacists had jobs or were in the military.

"Iva came here to the house one day really upset. Walked all the way here from town, mind you." He gave each man a solemn look before continuing. "Told me she was going to quit; she didn't want to work in the drug store anymore. I had a hard time getting her to tell me the problem. Julia, bless that dear woman's heart, took Iva into the bedroom and had a long talk with her. My Julia could always size up what was wrong. They came out and Iva calmly told me what was going on. The scoundrel wouldn't keep his hands off her. He threatened to fire her and have her old man arrested if she didn't cooperate.

"Well, he had no authority to fire anyone. However, I was still laid up and wasn't able to go back to work. I knew I likely wouldn't find another pharmacist if I fired him. Iva refused to continue to work at the drug store. The only thing I could do was to close the drug store which would hurt the town people."

Norm stopped and wiped his brow. As he continued his voice quivered, "Then my sweet Julia came up with a plan, bless her heart. She had a sister and brother-in-law who ran a dry cleaner in Detroit. Because of the war, they were forever having trouble finding enough help. Julia gave her sister a call and explained the situation. Janet, my sister-in-law, was overjoyed to get Iva's help. They even had a small apartment over their garage where Iva could live.

"The next day, Janet drove here and took Iva back to Detroit. Iva worked in the cleaners for many years. She even married one of the delivery drivers. They come to visit a couple of times a year. Julia and I used to go see them on occasion.

"So, Iva's not the skeleton, thank goodness. She'll be tickled though when I tell her!"

The four men ate Flora's lunch of ham and cheese sandwiches on rye bread, potato chips and sugar cookies for dessert. All four had been in World War I and understood how the horrible memories lingered. They were free to reminisce without criticism or disapproval. By four o'clock they were talked out; the three visitors got up to leave. Norm looked at Walt and Gully with just a hint of teary eyes, "Don't you two be strangers; I'll be here any time you want to visit." Both promised to come again, soon.

Chapter 18

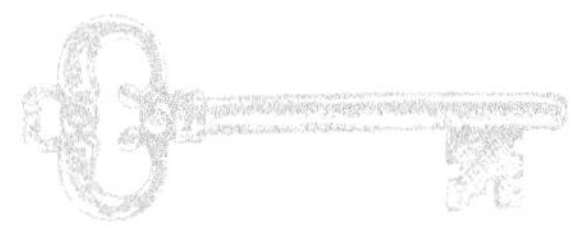

Betty's sixteenth birthday was in three days. She had begged for a big party with several of her friends invited. She started with asking to have five girlfriends over. It was now down to three. It was the custom of the Hunts to celebrate birthdays with only family. Judy did not feel up to entertaining a gang of teenagers nor did she want to change tradition. It would set a precedent and the other children would want big parties on their birthdays.

The celebrant was allowed to choose a favorite dinner. Grandma Hunt made the birthday cake, whatever flavor the birthday person requested. Grandpa and Grandma Hunt always came. The Seymours, Judy's parents, were also always invited. Judy's father usually came. Judy's mother did not like birthdays nor did she care much for children. She had never come to any of her grandchildren's birthday suppers.

Betty chose hamburgers for her dinner. She didn't care what else Judy prepared to go with them. She was upset about not getting a big party with her friends. She said she didn't care what kind of cake Grandma baked.

The night of Betty's birthday dinner, two of her very best friends arrived. Betty was surprised and a bit ashamed for acting so ill-tempered. She hugged her mother and told her she was sorry for how she had acted. Just before sitting down to eat, Judy's father walked in, followed by Harriet. Judy was so pleased, she thought she was going to cry.

After Betty had opened her presents, Lou took her aside. He handed her a set of car keys. "This Saturday, I'll take you for your driving test at the DMV in Flint. I know you'll pass. Driving is a great responsibility and can be taken away. We only have one car. You will be expected to help Mom with driving chores such as getting the younger kids to places and running errands. That's even when you don't want to. In her condition and at her age, she's going to need more help than usual. Can we count on you?"

Betty nodded several times, her eyes wide with excitement, "Yes Daddy. Oh yes!"

"One thing more, any tickets you get are your responsibility. I won't pay for them.

I expect you to drive the speed limit. Understand?"

Betty bobbed her head up and down, "Yes Daddy, thank you, thank you." She hugged her dad. Lou realized it had been a long time since they had hugged. It caused a lump in his throat.

The younger children went off to their affairs. Betty and her friends started to help with the dishes. Judy told them to sit down; the older women would clean up. Darlene wasn't sure what she was expected to do. Judy looked at her and smiled. "Why don't you come into the kitchen and put the dishes away as they're dried?" Darlene nodded.

Lou, his dad and father-in-law went outside to talk. After they left Grandma Hunt spoke, "I'm glad they left. Judy, I believe you have good wisdom and I need some advice. There's a problem I need your opinion on." This astonished and pleased Judy's mother, Harriet.

Judy stood in the middle of the kitchen with a dirty dish in each hand. "Thank you. That's very kind of you to say that."

Joan continued, "There's a situation at church. The Freeds are moving to Lansing. You know Inez Freed has taught the junior high girls' Sunday School class for several years. Mavis Hampton has volunteered to be the new teacher."

"Why that's wonderful. She'll be great, and the girls will love her."

"I agree, still there are a couple of ladies on the board who have misgivings."

"Hmmm, I bet I can guess who they are. Did they say why they don't want her to be the teacher?"

"There are a couple of reasons. For one, she's divorced."

Betty had been half listening to this conversation while she and her friends were looking at the high school yearbook. She got up from her chair and walked into the kitchen. "Mavis isn't divorced."

"Yes, she is, Dear."

"No, she isn't, Grandma. She told me the man she would have married died in Korea."

Harriet had been wiping the dishes as Joan washed, "Oh how sad. Were they engaged?'

"No, he died before they met."

The three women stopped what they were doing, looked at Betty and said in unison, "What?"

"Mavis said if he hadn't died, he would

have come home and they would have met, fallen in love and married. Because he died, they never got the chance."

"That's very interesting. Why does she let people think she's divorced?" asked Judy.

"She says she isn't responsible for what people think. Personally, I think letting people, especially women, believe she's divorced gives her a certain allure that helps her business."

"That's quite perceptive Betty", Harriet volunteered.

Joan continued, "Well, that eliminates one problem. There is still another."

Judy interrupted her mother-in-law, "Just a minute. It doesn't really. What if it were true that she's divorced? Why should that disqualify her? The important thing is, she has accepted Jesus as her Savior, and she is living a Godly life. We've both heard her testify in church about answers to prayers and how God has blessed her. She's a real Christian. We've all had to seek forgiveness. And thank God, when we do, He says He forgets our sins."

Betty told the ladies, "Y'know, sometimes when a lady comes in to get her hair done and has a problem, Mavis will stop right in the middle of doing her hair and pray. Other times, I've heard her promise to pray for one person or another, during her devotions before she goes to bed."

"Thank you for the information, both of you. If you don't mind, I'm going to use your words at the board meeting tomorrow night. I'm not going to mention the fact she's not divorced."

"You said there were two problems. What's the other one Grandma?"

"Some of the women don't like the way she dresses."

"Oh, for goodness sake! How petty can people be! If I had a figure like hers, I'd dress the same way. They're just jealous. It's a good thing I'm not on the board; I'd give those biddies a piece of my mind."

"Mother!" exclaimed Betty.

The next night Joan took a deep breath and squared her shoulders as she placed her hand on the church door knob ready to do battle. A still small voice whispered in her ear, "Joan be nice". She entered the meeting room, smiled and said hello to the other board members as she took a seat.

The Sunday school director opened the meeting with prayer and began covering the agenda. Finally, he presented the item most were waiting for. "As you all know

Mavis Hampton has volunteered to be the junior high teacher. The meeting is open for discussion."

Before the director had a chance to sit down, Joan stood and began to talk. "There are some things I want to say about Mavis. Everyone here has heard Mavis testify in church. She has been faithful in helping with funeral dinners and taking meals to the sick."

Joan looked directly at one of the ladies, "Vivian, I seem to remember when Bill was hurt on the job; you had to go back to work. Wasn't it Mavis who loaned you her typewriter and adding machine so you could practice your skills? And the day of your interview, didn't she have you come to her shop to do your hair and even loaned you a smart outfit to wear? My granddaughter told me she sometimes stops in the middle of doing a customer's hair to pray about a problem the patron is having."

Next Joan centered on an older gentleman, "Carl, remember when your Edna was so ill? Didn't Mavis come almost every day to bathe your wife and change her bedding? I seem to remember on some days she stayed for a couple of hours so you would have time to yourself. This was after she had been working on her feet all day.

"For the two weeks of Vacation Bible School each summer, she only schedules evening appointments so she can help during the mornings. Probably each one of us could recall something good, Mavis has done. There is no doubt in my mind she is a good Christian."

The director asked if anyone else wanted to speak. No one did. The vote was a unanimous yes.

Chapter 19

Beverly Gullington finally tracked down Edith Campbell, now Edith Smith. She telephoned Edith. She and her husband had turned over the operation of their pig farm to their daughter and the daughter's husband five years earlier. The Smiths now lived in Battle Creek near another daughter.

Edith couldn't remember who Beverly was. Beverly patiently explained several times that she used to be Beverly Morrison, and her family had lived down the road from the Campbells. Bev said, "Edith, remember your sister Anita and I were best friends? I was over at your house all the time."

Edith finally said yes, she thought she remembered some Morrisons living a ways down the road from her family. She couldn't quite understand why Beverly was calling her. Bev decided Edith was getting senile. Perhaps trying to get information from her would be a waste of time; but she had to try. Bev offered to drive to Battle Creek for a visit. Edith hesitated before saying, "Let me talk to my husband and call you back." Bev gave Edith her telephone number which she had to repeat four times, before Edith got it right.

Two days later Bev picked up the receiver of the ringing telephone. At the other end was a male voice. "Hello, this is Nate Smith, Edith's husband. Is this Beverly?"

"Yes, it is, Mr. Smith. Thank you so much for returning my call."

"Well, I'm not sure what you want. You probably guessed Edith is having a little trouble understanding people and remembering things. Who are you, and why exactly did you call? If you're selling anything, we're not interested."

"Oh no, Mr. Smith I'm not a salesman. I used to live on the next farm across the road and a bit south of the Campbell's. In the 20's, I moved away and married. When my husband retired from the Army, we decided to settle in Leichester. I got to thinking about old times. Anita Campbell and I were friends and I wondered what became of her and her sisters. After their father died, the sisters, who weren't married moved away with their mother." Bev waited for Nate to respond.

"How long have you been living in Leichester?"

Bev felt a bit embarrassed to answer. She finally said, "Since 1957."

"Almost ten years! Lady, what's this all about?"

Bev sighed, then finally told the truth. "Several weeks ago, a skeleton was discovered in the old house where the Campbells once lived. We believe it is that of a woman. We're trying to identify any women who have gone missing in the past fifty years."

"Lady, you sound crazy. I've never heard of any skeleton in any attic. Are you trying to say it could be one of my sisters-in-law? Are you from the police?"

"I'm not officially with the police. You might call me a volunteer investigator. I know there were six Campbell girls. Please be so kind as to tell me what became of each. I just want to rule them off our list.”

“You sound as batty as my wife. All my sisters-in-law are present and accounted for! If the police have any questions, you tell them to contact me, not some unofficial volunteer investigator!” Nate Smith slammed down the receiver.

Bev sat looking at the telephone, “Well, that certainly didn’t go as I expected.”

Chapter 20

The county store owners were having their July meeting. After the routine business the president, Sterling Dean, owner of the Wellington Hardware Store, cleared his throat and looked about the room. "Gentlemen and ladies, I have some sorry business to present. There is a two-hundred-fifty-dollar shortage in our treasury." A collective gasp was emitted around the room, then several people spoke at the same time, most asking how this could be. Never in the one hundred plus year history of the county store owners' association had anything like this happened before.

Sterling held up his hands asking for silence. He beckoned for Jeffrey Drake, the treasurer, to come to the front. Jeffrey approached the front while wringing his hands. He stood with a dejected look on his face. Jeffrey had owned the only men's clothing store in the county. The store had been in business since 1882. It had recently suffered a fire. Sterling sat down as Jeffrey began to speak, "I'm so sorry. It's all my fault. I did a terrible thing. I'm ashamed to tell you what I did."

Eber Plait, the oldest member and owner of the feed store, shouted, "Come on man, speak up. I can't hear you. It's getting late. I want to go home and go to bed. What happened to the money?"

"I borrowed it to buy some stock for my

store, and then I had that fire in March. I hadn't paid my insurance because I was so short of money. If the fire hadn't happened, I would have had the money to put back and no one would have known. I'm sorry, I'm so sorry. I planned to resign as treasurer because I don't have a business anymore. I had to find a new job. Right now, I'm stocking shelves at that new department store in Flint at night. I intend to repay." He sat slumped into a nearby chair and hung his head.

"Should we tell the sheriff?" inquired Lawrence Pearson, the owner of the Tip Top Bakery.

"I didn't think things like that happened in this county," declared an indignant Roger Goodman, pharmacist of the Rexall® Drug Store.

"What should we do? How do we get

our money back?" asked Rebecca Cole, proprietor of the ladies' dress shop in Leichester. Silence filled the room for several minutes.

Mavis stood and tapped her pencil on the table. "I have an idea. Let's have a community fair."

"A what?" asked Eber. "That sounds just like a woman."

"Now let's hear Mavis out. I didn't hear anyone else coming up with an idea. Tell us what you're thinking Mavis," put in Rebecca.

"We could hold a fair of an afternoon at the park. Each store owner could have a booth. For example, Eber, you have a couple of ponies. You could charge children to ride. I'm sure if we tried, each of us could come up with some kind of activity that would raise money. We could even charge a few dollars to people in the county, who would like to set up their own booths to sell things like homemade jams or crafts." She sat down. The room was quiet while each person contemplated the idea.

At length several people began to talk. A motion was made and passed to have a fair. A planning committee was formed.

The morning of the fair, August 15, Judy dropped Betty off at Tangles. She and Mavis were to operate an ice cream stand. Betty walked into the shop and froze. Mavis looked spectacular from her head to her shoes. Her blonde hair was curled and drawn up above her ears by a wide red ribbon. She had on a snug sleeveless white blouse with red polka dots. The first three buttons were unfastened, exposing a generous amount of cleavage. Cinched around her slim waist was a wide black belt separating the blouse from a red, tight, and short pencil skirt. Straw mules with red flowers adorned her feet.

Betty felt like Cinderella. She had chosen to wear a plain white blouse, yellow petal pushers and tennis shoes. Her hair was in a ponytail secured by a rubber band. "Mavis, you look wonderful!"

Mavis smiled her sweet, shy smile while appraising Betty. "Hmm, would you like me to see what I can do to gussy you up a bit?"

"Oh yes! Please!"

Mavis approached Betty and pulled out the hem of her blouse from the petal pushers. She undid the two bottom buttons and tied the ends together in a bow around Betty's midriff. "Sit in my chair, I'll be right back."

Mavis left and hurried up the stairs to her bedroom.

Betty sat in the styling chair and looked in the mirror. Wide-spaced light gray eyes stared back at her. Her perfectly oval face had high cheek bones with a very round chin. Most people said she looked like her Grandmother Seymour. Betty thought, "Am I pretty?" She didn't like her thin lips; it was hardly worth using lipstick. Her smooth porcelain skin which seldom had a blemish was the envy of her teen-age friends.

Mavis returned with three scatter pins. They were kittens in various positions, one was holding a ball, another standing on its hind legs and the third, curled up as if sleeping. "Pin these on your blouse. No, not so high! A little lower towards your bosom. That's good." Next Mavis handed Betty a pair of white sandals. "Put these on. They may be a little big, but it won't matter as they're open at the toes and heels.

"Now let's see what we can do with your hair." She took out the rubber band and began brushing. As Mavis worked on Betty's hair she talked, "Such lovely color, brown with hints of auburn. Women pay a lot of money to get this color." When she was finished, she twirled Betty around and handed her a mirror. Mavis had put the hair into a French twist. Adorned on one side of the twist were yellow flowers. Mavis started pulling out strands of hair from each side and from the front of Betty's face. She dampened these, twisted them into curls and secured each curl with clips. "Leave the clips in until we get to the park. Then pull them out. Don't do anything to the curls. They'll just hang."

Several booths were already set up by the time Mavis and Betty arrived. There was a dunking tank, where several county officials volunteered to take turns being the dunkees. Eber Plait was getting his ponies ready. Lawrence Pearson, the baker, had a cake walk set up. But, instead of whole cakes, he was only giving out cupcakes. The dress shop owner, Rebecca Cole made a "roulette" wheel with prizes at each stop. Altogether twelve booths were scattered around the park. Several nonmembers had paid to set up their own craft and food booths. The fair was to run from 10:30 a.m. to 3:00 p.m.

Mavis and Betty prepared their ice cream stand for customers. Betty was to take the money; Mavis would dip the ice cream. When the fair started, Mavis placed the ice cream containers on low stools. Betty watched as Mavis served the ice cream.

She placed one foot on a stool rung while smiling at the customer. She leaned over the container and slowly scooped a generous portion onto the cone, then handed it to the grinning customer.

Betty understood for the first time the sexual power women had over men. A goodly number of men returned two and even three times for ice cream. Eighty-one-year-old, Hank Lyle said with a grin on his face, "I can't remember when I've ever eaten so much ice cream." Several groups of men congregated under a tree within view of Mavis. Teenage boys buzzed around Betty. A number of women tut-tutted and tossed back their heads as they cast unapproving glares at the ice cream booth.

Two old codgers were sitting on a bench a short distance away. They were watching the young men and some not so young men, buy scoop after scoop of ice cream. Tobias Ashton, the older of the two men looked at his old friend, "Jake, do you remember when the Rialto started showing those silent moving pictures back in the '20's?"

"Sure, I do. The first time my ma took me, I thought they were magic."

"Well, those whipper-snappers buying that ice cream remind me of a story I heard. There was a man that kept going to the same silent movie show. In the movie a group of young gals were on the far side of some railroad tracks. They were disrobing to go swimming. Just as they got down to the essentials, a train came by blocking the movie goers' view. By the time the caboose cleared the tracks, the gals were all in the water. When asked why he kept going to the same show day after day, he replied, 'That train can't be on schedule every time!'" Both men laughed at Tobias's story.

"Those fellows, buying that ice cream are hoping, just once, they might get a glimpse of a little more than what Mavis wants to show."

Jake chuckled, "You're right Tobias. You're sure fired right!"

By one-thirty, the ice cream was running low. Mavis caught the attention of Roger Goodman, owner of the Rexall® Drug Store. She told him about the problem. He drove to his store and brought back more ice cream from his soda fountain.

The Tip Top Bakery was also doing a rousing business, especially with the children. It cost five cents to enter the game. A large round table was set up with eight cardboard cupcakes placed equal distances around the edge of the table. The game started with each of eight people standing beside a cupcake. Before the music started one cupcake was removed. As music played, people walked around the table. When the music stopped the person left standing with no cupcake was out of the game. Another cupcake was removed. This continued until only one cupcake was left. The last time the music stopped, the person standing beside the one remaining cupcake won a real cupcake.

Like the ice cream concession, Mr. Lawrence was running low on real cupcakes. He continued the game by giving IOU's to the winners. They could come by the bakery to pick up their cupcakes. Mr. Lawrence decided, he would only use IOU's next year, if the association had another fair. When people came in to claim their prizes, chances are they might buy something more.

Louis played the game eleven times before winning a cupcake. When Lou found out he laughed. He told his son he could have bought two or three cupcakes for the fifty-five cents it had cost to play eleven times. Louis said, "I don't care. It's the thrill of winning that counts!"

The county store owners association made more than four hundred dollars in profit. The ice cream stand made the most. The Tip Top Bakery came in second. There was talk of making the fair an annual event.

Sean O'Toole was at the fair all day. He was unofficially "keeping an eye on activities," including the ice cream stand. He approached Mavis and offered to help clean up. She hadn't taken time to eat lunch and was not only hungry but also tired. She welcomed his help. When all their work was finished, Sean suggested, "How about I follow you ladies back to the beauty shop? Once we get this stuff put away, it'll be my treat for dinner."

"That sounds lovely, don't you think so Betty?"

Betty had been thinking all the while they were cleaning up, "It's not really me Sean is interested in; it's Mavis". Out loud she said, "I'm pretty much done in. If you don't mind, I'd just as soon you dropped me off at home." In truth she really wanted to go with them.

Mavis and Betty got into Sean's car after putting things away at the beauty shop. They drove to the Hunt farm and let Betty out. Judy was surprised to see her oldest come in. "I thought you and Mavis were going out to supper after the fair."

"We were, except Sean came by our booth, helped us clean up and offered to take us out. I told them I didn't want to go."

"Why did you say that?"

"Mother, 'two's company, three's a crowd'."

Watching Betty rummage through the refrigerator for something to eat, Judy realized Betty was growing up in more ways than just physically.

Mavis and Sean became the talk of the town. Most people thought Mavis was at least six or seven years older than Sean. In actual fact, Mavis was twenty-eight and Sean was near twenty-six. Mavis began setting her appointments so she would be free on Sean's days off. They enjoyed each other's company, becoming good friends and falling in love. When Sean was able, he helped Mavis in her Sunday School Class. One Sunday, she stood off to one side and thought to herself, "He's really very good with children."

Chapter 21

Len Rheimes the only remaining criminal from the botched Smitty robbery continued to dodge the authorities by various ploys. Occasionally he had gone into the houses of people who were not home to get food. No one, it seemed, ever locked their doors. In one house he had found an old gun under a pile of rags. He couldn't find any bullets. He took the gun anyway.

Once he watched a family as they packed for a vacation. When they left, he stayed in the house five days. He slept in one of the kid's beds and used the bath tub. He stuffed the dirty towel and wash cloth he had used back in the corner of the kid's closet. He figured once the mother found the dirty linen, she would blame the kid.

Presently he was staying in a swell camp area in the midst of a corn field now that the stalks had reached their full height. The only way anyone could see him was by flying over. He tried eating the field corn. Even as hungry as he was, he just couldn't stomach it. Soon the corn would be fully ripened and the picking would begin. Len realized it wouldn't be long before he would have to leave his corn field camp and find another place to hide.

Out her breakfast room window, Harriet watched a farmer bailing hay. It had been almost two months since she had contacted the school principal. She began to wonder if she was ever going to receive a telephone number or address for Eleanor Hanover. She hoped Eleanor could shine some light on what happened to Alice Higgins. Finally, one afternoon at the end of August, the telephone rang. Harriet's maid, Flora, answered, "Hello, Seymour residence."

"This is Eleanor Hanover. May I speak to Harriet Seymour please? "

Flora rested the receiver on the table and hurried to tell her employer. She had overheard Mr. and Mrs. Seymour talking about "the skeleton" and knew Harriet was anxious to hear from this woman.

"Hello, this is Harriet Seymour. Is this Eleanor Hanover?"

"Yes, Miss Perry wrote me that you wanted to talk to me about Alice Higgins. Why is that?"

"Alice and I worked together at the hospital. She just disappeared one day. I was so mad at her for leaving me in a bind. But I've always wondered what happened to her."

"You've waited over twenty years to find out?"

"Well yes, however, there is a particular reason. As I said, I was very angry with her for the vanishing act she pulled. I tried to just put it out of my mind and moved on."

Harriet hesitated to say more. How could she diplomatically tell this woman on the other end of the line, she thought Alice might be a skeleton? Harriet decided to side step Eleanor's comment, "Do you know how I can reach Alice. It's important."

"If I can get in touch with Alice and she

agrees to see you, would you be willing to come to Detroit?"

"Yes", answered Harriet quickly. "I'll come any day and any time she is available." Harriet made the quick decision, if she had a conflict, she'd change whatever other appointment she had.

Eleanor said she would be in touch with Harriet. Harriet sat back in her chair feeling very satisfied with herself. She always enjoyed going to Detroit. She would make a day of it; shopping at Hudson's and even eating lunch at the London Chop House.

Harriet felt powerless waiting for Eleanor to call her back. Then, at last, Eleanor telephoned. She asked Harriet to come to her house in Detroit at two o'clock on Tuesday, September seventh. Before leaving, Harriet's husband Martin told her, he, Gully and Walt were having lunch together to discuss the information which had been discovered. Harriet recommended the men put off their discussion until the women could meet with them. She suggested everyone come to their house for supper this Thursday. Martin was stunned. Such an invitation was so out of character for Harriet. He promised to talk to the men about the supper.

As she watched the fallen leaves dance across the road, Harriet thought, "It's going to be an early winter this year. I wonder if that means a bad winter?" From when it had first opened, she had never driven on the new interstate Highway 75. Her way took longer, but she didn't care. She was not a fast driver and the traffic, whizzing past her the couple of times she tried driving on other interstates, unnerved her. Her appointment was for two o'clock.

After purchasing a new hat at Hudson's Department Store and enjoying a light lunch at the London Chop House Restaurant, Harriet arrived promptly at two. She was always on time, detesting being late or people who arrived late. In Harriet's opinion, once in a while, something might cause a person to be late for an appointment. She believed being habitually late was a form of manipulation and control.

Pulling into the driveway, she noticed a rather old Pontiac, bearing an Indiana license plate. "Interesting", she thought. The front door to the house opened as she climbed the porch steps.

"Good afternoon, I'm Eleanor Hanover. You must be Harriet Seymour." Harriet smiled and nodded. "Please come in, Mrs. Seymour."

Harriet knew she was making an impression in her cream-colored linen suit and Jackie Kennedy-style pill box hat. Her large brown straw clutch bag and heels matched perfectly. She took two steps into the homey, green-wallpapered living room and stopped short. The fixed smile on her face faded as her hand went to her chest and she gasped. Sitting on the dark brown sofa was Alice, a bit older looking and much heavier, but it was Alice Higgins. "Alice, I'm glad we could finally meet again."

Eleanor spoke as Alice stood to meet Harriet, "Mrs. Seymour, would you care for something to drink, coffee, iced tea or a pop?"

Harriet sank into a much-used arm chair, "No, thank you." Eleanor quietly left the room.

Before Harriet could say anything, Alice began to talk, "Harriet, I'm so sorry for walking out on you that night, so many years ago."

"All these years I've resented your leaving me in the lurch. I've gone over and over in my mind what I'd say to you if ever I met you again. Now I don't know what to say."

"Please forgive me, if you can. I know, as a nurse it was a terrible thing to do."

"The Director of Nursing told me you were fired for doing that, as you should have been!"

"Yes, I was. Please, let me tell you what happened."

Harriet leaned back in the chair and crossed her arms. "Go ahead. I'd like to hear this."

"You probably remember, it was the day of Michael's funeral that I didn't show up for work. I was so overcome that I sat by myself, at the back of the church during the service. I just couldn't bring myself to go to the cemetery or the dinner. I didn't want to go on living. I bought some sleeping pills and a bottle of whiskey. I planned to kill myself. I drove out to the old Hunt house. Mike had been trying to get his dad to let us move there after we got married. We often went there to sit on the porch swing, dreaming about our lives together.

"It got very dark that night; there was no moon. I took the top off the bottle of whiskey and had several pills in my hand. Then, I remembered something you had once told a patient."

"Something I said?"

"Yes, we had a young girl only about

seventeen. She had tried to commit suicide. I don't even remember why, yet I did remember what you told her. 'Suicide is a permanent solution to a temporary problem.' That's what you said."

"Well, that wasn't original with me. I first heard it from an instructor while in nurses' training."

"I'm glad you remembered it. Anyway, I debated back and forth with myself. One side of me said this wasn't a temporary problem. Mike was killed in training and he was never coming back. Another side of me said even though that was true, I could get through it.

"For the first time in many years, I prayed. I told God if He would help me get past this horrible experience, I'd do whatever He wanted me to do."

"Did He?"

"Yes, He did. I got in my car and drove home to Indiana. The next day I called the hospital and talked to the director. She said, I didn't deserve any sympathy or consideration; other women, some married with children, were facing the same grief. She fired me on the spot. She also threatened to get my nursing license revoked.

"After hanging up I wasn't upset. I told God if this was what He wanted to happen, I'd accept it."

"Did you lose your license?"

"No, I never heard from her again, or the State Board of Licensing. I took a job at the veterans' hospital near where I lived. I thought it would be emotionally hard working there. And it was. It was also healing."

"Did you ever marry?"

"Yes, ten years ago I married a very gentle, quiet man, totally different from Mike. We have two sons. Mike will always have a place in my heart. Someday I'll see him in Heaven and we'll walk together beside the River of Life. I truly love my husband and I thank God every day for my family."

Harriet looked Alice in the eye, "I really mean this, I'm glad you found peace. So many people search all their lives and never find it. The anger I've held for so long, for all these years is gone."

"Thank you, Harriet."

Both women sat looking at each other. Gazing questioningly at Harriet, Alice stated, "I still don't understand why you wanted to find me after all these years."

Harriet hesitated before answering, not sure what to say. "My daughter, Judy, and her family now live in the Hunt house. It still belongs to Mike's father. The attic openings had been nailed shut for all the time they've lived there. A couple of months ago, my grandchildren worked one of the doors to the attic open and found the skeleton of a woman. I told Judy I'd try to locate you to rule you out as the skeleton."

Alice began to laugh to such an extreme, Eleanor came running into the living room. "What's the matter? Is something wrong?"

Alice was wiping tears from her eyes, "Things are just fine. I'm alive, and all is well."

Harriet stood up and gave Alice a genuine smile, and so unlike her, a small hug, "I need to be going. I hope to get out of town before the factory traffic starts. I'm glad you're not the skeleton in the attic."

"Me too. I could never understand why Mr. Hunt was so reluctant about our moving in. When you find out who it is, will you let me know?"

"Yes, give me your telephone number and I will."

Harriet heard Eleanor asking as she left, "What did she mean a skeleton in the attic?"

Driving home Harriet was troubled by two things. First, her brother had been reported missing in action in World War II. The family hoped and prayed he would be coming home with prisoners of war. He was not among them. For years, Harriet's mother had fantasized that he had a head injury and was in a veterans' hospital, insensible. She went to her grave with no closure, always wondering what had happened to her only son. Thinking about the skeleton, Harriet wondered, if another mother had gone to her grave sorrowing about a child who had never come home.

Harriet could not remember the last time she had prayed. She felt she should and yet she didn't actually know what to pray about. She simply asked God to comfort those mothers grieving for lost children and thanked Him for her daughter and grandchildren.

The second point that bothered Harriet was the statement Alice had made, "I could never understand why Mr. Hunt was so reluctant about our moving in." Harriet wondered, "Did Steve Hunt know more about the skeleton than he would admit?"

Harriet couldn't get Alice's remark out of her mind. On her way home she decided to visit the sheriff's office. The officer on duty was so surprised to see her, he was tongue-tied. He went into Sheriff Byrne's inner office to tell him Mrs. Seymour wanted to see him. Dave came out to the main area and welcomed Harriet. He asked her to come into his office. At first Harriet wondered if her visit was frivolous. However, when she told him of her trip to Detroit and what Alice had said, Dave seemed very interested. He said, "Mrs. Seymour, do you know you are interfering in a criminal investigation?"

"Why no, I didn't David."

"Walter Hunt and the rest of his 'gang' were told to stop asking questions. That includes you."

"Well! I'm sorry, I thought I was helping. And I'm not in his gang!" Harriet got up to leave.

Sheriff Byrne also stood, "I'm sorry Mrs. Seymour, I didn't mean to be rude or impolite. This information you've just told me is important. Please understand, we may be dealing with a murderer. If he's still alive, he may not take kindly to amateur interference. I just don't want anyone to get hurt. Please let us handle the investigation."

"From now on, I'm finished with asking questions. Besides, I doubt if there is anything else I could learn anyway. I found out more than I thought I ever would, talking to my old friend."

Harriet left the Sheriff's Office and walked to her car. She smiled as she got in and went home.

Chapter 22

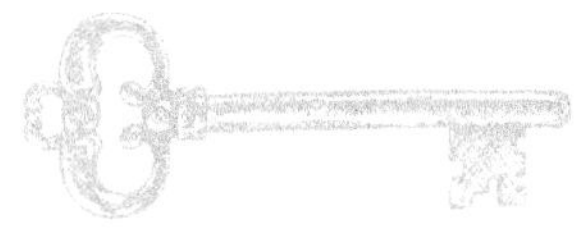

Walt, Gully and Martin met at **Aunt Patti's Kitchen** for lunch. They decided that having a group meeting to review the information each person had learned was a good idea. Martin relayed Harriet's offer to host a supper.

Joan and Beverly both offered to bring a dish. Harriet really didn't want any dishes brought. She wanted to control what was on the menu. However, neither did she want to offend her new friends by sounding pompous. She told Joan to bring a dessert and Beverly to bring a fruit salad.

The night of the dinner meeting Walt and Joan traveled about half way when Joan cried out, "The dessert! We forgot the dessert. Turn around."

Walt made a U-turn and headed back. He pulled into the driveway and waited in the car while Joan headed for the kitchen door. She had no more than put her hand on the door knob, when a figure dressed in dark clothes rushed out of the house. The person pushed Joan and continued to run past the car and down the drive to the street.

The house was built at the top of a slight hill with a small pond at the bottom. Joan was knocked to the ground and rolled down the lawn, over and over like a log. There was a large stump at the side of the pond. Her head hit the edge of the stump as she rolled into the cold water. She was dazed and it took her a minute to realize what had happened. All at once, Joan felt strong arms lifting her up out of the water.

Walt set her gently on the dew-dampened grass. She was shivering more from shock than cold. Walt removed his jacket and put it around her. "Help me up; I want to get up."

"Are you sure Sweetheart? Maybe I should call an ambulance. You might have some broken bones and your head is bleeding."

Joan moved her arms and legs. "There's nothing broken. Just help me up." Walt gingerly lifted his wife. Every part of her body hurt, still she was sure nothing was broken. He held her close as they walked up the hill to the house.

"Let me take you next door to the Millers.

I'm calling the sheriff. Someone could still be in the house."

Sheriff David Byrne lived two blocks north of the Hunts. When he heard the call come in, he jumped in his car and drove to the Hunts. The duty deputy, Ron Simmons, arrived two minutes after David. Walt was standing in the drive waiting. He explained what had happened.

David went next door to see Joan while Deputy Simmons stood keeping the Hunt residence under surveillance. The sheriff encouraged Joan to go to the emergency room, but she refused. Sheriff Byrne knew Mrs. Miller was a registered nurse. He decided she would see to the care of Joan. He left the house with Mrs. Miller hovering over Joan.

The sheriff told Deputy Simmons to go around to the front door and enter. Dave entered by the kitchen door. They searched both floors of the house, the basement and garage but found no one. Dave asked Walt to come in to have a look around for anything missing. A desk in the kitchen was the only area in disarray. Both men realized the intruder was probably looking for any incriminating evidence that could link him to the skeleton.

Sheriff Byrne decided it was time to put an end to the amateur sleuthing. The next morning, he told the secretary, Thelma, to call Walter Hunt. He wanted to have a meeting at the Hunts about three o'clock. Walt said it would be okay. She then called Mr. and Mrs. Gullington and Mr. and Mrs. Seymour to have them at the Hunts' at three.

Each couple arrived as requested. Joan had coffee ready and a luscious looking lemon meringue pie. It was the dessert she had planned to take to the supper last night.

Sheriff Byrne had a difficult time getting the couples to focus. At first, they were very solicitous to Joan, asking her all kinds of questions about the intruder. Then Joan apologized over and over again to Harriet for spoiling the supper, as if it were her fault for being attacked. Next, everyone made over the pie. Joan said it had to be eaten, as lemon pie didn't keep well. Bev offered to cut the pie. She expertly cut it into seven pieces. Sheriff Byrne at first refused a piece. Joan eventually coaxed him into having a piece. Before the sheriff could get the couples quiet, second cups of coffee were served.

Finally, he raised his hands for quiet, "Thank you for coming on short notice.

Mrs. Hunt, are you feeling okay?" Joan smiled and nodded. "I thought it would be easier on you having this meeting here instead of asking you to come to the office. I didn't expect you to have refreshments ready but the pie was very good."

"Oh David, it was no trouble. The lemon pie was for last night. I already had it made and I feel just fine." In truth, she had a terrible headache and every muscle in her body was protesting. "Are we in trouble?"

"No, no one is in trouble, exactly. You all do understand you were asked to stop investigating. It is not safe, as proven by the break-in last night."

Gully declared, "Sheriff, we were only trying to help. We know you don't really have the manpower you need to protect this whole county with none of the towns having their own police force. Added to that is the robbery and killing at Smitty's Beer Garden last spring."

 "We thought we were doing you a favor," Bev added.

Walt spoke, "Yeah, nothing's been done about finding who the woman in the attic was and what happened to her."

"There you are wrong. We take all unexplained deaths seriously. We and the State Police have been investigating. And even if we hadn't, it would not be your place to do so."

"Well, why haven't we heard anything?" responded Gully.

"It is not our responsibility to report what we have uncovered to you. Since you have taken it upon yourselves to become involved, I will tell you this. The skeleton is of a man, not a woman."

"What!""You don't say!""That can't be!""Oh my!""Well, I'll be.""For goodness sake." These comments were expressed around the table all at the same time.

"Furthermore, the state medical examiner believes his death was the result of exsanguination."

"For crying out loud Sheriff, who do you think we are, a bunch of doctors? Speak English," complained Gully.

"Exsanguination means loss of blood. He was likely shot in the groin. The bullet hit the femoral artery and he bled to death."

Bev tipped her head to one side, wrinkled her brow and asked, "How do they know that? I thought it was only a skeleton."

"His right femur was shattered. Sean O'Toole found a bullet the first time he inspected the area. Also, there were a large number of rags covered with dried blood. He may have been strangled after he was shot, or the rope was around his neck for another reason. The medical examiner said he does not believe the man died from being strangled."

"It appears we have been wasting our time these past few months," voiced Bev.

"I don't feel I have. It's been a good experience for me. I made contact with an old acquaintance that I really disliked. Now that I've talked to her, I feel much differently about what happened. Also, I have such a different opinion about Judy marrying Lou. I see how wrong I was." Harriet said this as she smiled at Joan.

"I've found a new friend in Norm, the old pharmacist, and I plan to keep in regular touch with him." This was shared by Gully as he patted his wife's hand.

"And I think it has been rather exciting and interesting even if I did get pushed into the pond," added Joan.

"Well, I for one, agree with Dave. I was so scared last night as I watched Joan roll down that hill. I would've given anything not to have had it happen. I feel guilty about the whole affair." Walt looked at his wife in utter distress.

Joan smiled her sweet smile and took Walt's hand. "It's all right Darling, God looked after me."

Chapter 23

While the group were still talking, Dave left the house and headed back to his office. He was stopped at a red light at Peacock and Roseland. Waiting in the opposite direction, he saw Lou in his truck. Dave made a U-turn when the light changed. Cars in front of him began to pull to the side of the road when he turned on his emergency light. Lou saw the flashing red light and pulled to the side of the road. Dave pulled in behind him and got out. Lou waited in his truck until he recognized Dave then he also got out.

"Hi Dave, was I doing something wrong?"

"Nothing's wrong. I want to ask you a couple of questions about the openings to the attic. I can't get it clear about the openings being blocked."

"Didn't my uncle tell you he nailed them shut?"

"No, the deputy who interviewed him wrote in his report that your uncle didn't know anything about them being sealed."

"That's not true. Judy, Betty and I were living in a small one-bedroom apartment, and Judy was expecting our second baby. We had to have a bigger place. Houses were in high demand and in short supply. That large house was just sitting empty. Several times I asked my Uncle Steve to let us rent it and move in.

"Finally, after almost begging him, he gave

in. He took me around the house showing me different things. When we came to the bedroom, that is now Connie's and Gloria's, he opened the closet door and pointed to the access, saying, 'I've nailed shut the opening to the attic. There's no reason for anyone to go up there. I have some valuable things stored there, and I don't want anyone getting into them.' I just figured he meant antiques and such."

"It sounds like I need to have another talk with your uncle."

"You should know he's really sick and won't go to the doctor. My dad and I take turns going to see him a couple of times a week. He can hardly get out of bed. All he does is yell and tell us to leave him alone."

"Do you know if your uncle owns a gun?"

"He used to. It's a Mauser Automatic. He

took it off a dead German officer in World War I. He let Mike and me fire it a couple of times."

"That fits."

"Fits what?"

"Your skeleton is a man not a woman and probably bled to death from a gunshot wound to the femoral artery." Pointing to his leg Dave said, "It's in the leg. Sean found a spent bullet the first day he was in the attic examining the skeleton. The type of bullet Sean found is just like the ones used in a Luger."

"What about the rope? The kids said there was a rope around the neck bones."

"The rope seems to have been just window dressing. I need to go see Steve."

"Do you want me to go with you? I was on my way home. I've been late before."

"Sure, I'd really appreciate that. You go ahead and I'll follow."

Lou knocked on the front door several times. There was no answer. He had a key to his uncle's house which he then used to enter. Dave followed Lou into the house. Only the light coming in from the front door helped them see into the living room. Green World War II type blackout shades were pulled down over the windows. Lou called out to his uncle with no response. He looked in the front bedroom where Steve slept. He was not there. They walked into the dining room. It led from the living room to the kitchen. The shades in this room were also pulled. Lou looked into the kitchen and saw his uncle on the floor.

"Uncle Steve!"

The old man was lying on his side with his eyes closed. He opened them and looked at Lou. In a weak, halting voice he whispered, "Oh, Louis, help me, I hurt so much. Please do something."

Dave asked, "Where's the phone? I'll call an ambulance."

"On the counter, next to the back door. Take it easy Uncle Steve. We'll help you."

"Water, please, I need some water."

Lou hurried to the sink and filled a dirty glass he found sitting on the counter with water.

At the hospital a physician ordered oxygen and an I. V. for Steven Hunt. He was examined by a surgeon who ordered the patient to be taken directly into O. R. Lou called his folks to tell them about his uncle. He then called Judy to let her know what was happening, and that he would not be home for supper and to pray for Steve.

Walter and Joan arrived. It was only a short while when the surgeon came out to talk to the family. He informed them Steve had cancer throughout most of his body and would not live long. The best that could be done was to keep him comfortable and out of pain. He would be in recovery for at least another hour before going to a room.

Lou decided to go home. Judy would be anxious to learn how Lou's uncle was. Dave met Lou outside and asked him to come back to his uncle's house to have a look around. They looked through cupboards, closets, the dining room buffet and kitchen drawers. No gun was found.

"Lou, is there any place else he might have hidden the gun?"

"There's a shed in the back where the lawn mower and other yard equipment are kept."

The two men walked to the shed. Dave had a flash light he used to look around. The two men looked on shelves and in an old cabinet with broken glass doors. No gun was found.

Lou exited the shed and stopped just outside the door. Dave bumped into him not expecting Lou to be standing so close to the entrance. "What is it, Lou?"

"See that tree by the fence?"

"Yeah."

"Notice there's not another tree of any kind or shrub in the yard?" My uncle detested planting anything that could not be eaten. He said it was a waste of money and effort. He even despised having to care for grass. For my eighth birthday, my folks gave me a Schwinn® bicycle. Mike had taught me to ride using his bike. So, I rode over here to show Mike my new bike.

"Uncle Steve was here in the backyard planting this tree. He was real upset, yelling at me to git and go home. It had been a really dry summer. I thought it was strange planting a tree in August, especially knowing how he felt about growing something that couldn't be eaten. He'd have to use a lot of water on that tree to keep it from dying."

"Are you thinking your uncle might have placed the gun in the hole before planting the tree?"

"The way things are turning out, I guess it's possible. I'm trying to think of who he would have killed."

"I don't know. The strange thing is we

searched the records all the way back to 1930. Any man or boy who went missing during that time has been accounted for. Some kids took off for a while but always came back home. I'll get a crew out here tomorrow morning and have the tree dug up."

Lou locked up and the two went to their respective homes.

The next morning, Dave was watching as the tree was cut down. The stump was chained to a farm tractor and pulled out. Two men were down in the hole using shovels to dig around in the dirt. One man reached down then held up a rusty gun. "Is this what you're looking for Sheriff?"

Chapter 24

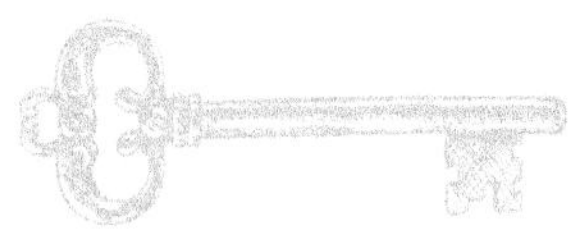

A week later, the Sheriff's secretary, Thelma took a call from a hospital nurse. Steve Hunt wanted to see the sheriff. Thelma said she would relay the message. At the moment, David and two deputies were trying to restrain a very agitated and disoriented man. They were waiting for Dr. Tucker to arrive to medicate him. Then he could be transferred to the hospital for evaluation.

Thelma gave David the message, after the agitated man was sedated and transferred.

Byrne figured he knew why Steve Hunt wanted to talk to him.

The sheriff waited by the unoccupied nurses' station a couple of minutes. R.N. Sissy Bennett came out of a patient's room carrying a handful of medical equipment. Sissy lived two houses south of Dave.

"Hi Dave, I'm glad you're here. Mr. Hunt has asked for you constantly. He's tried to pull out his tubes twice. He says he doesn't want them. He just wants to die. Dr. Tucker was here early this morning and at lunch time. And here he comes again."

Dr. Tucker exhaustedly walked up to the nurses' station. "Well, hello again Dave. I take it you're here to see Steve Hunt. Dave nodded. "Go on in, he wants to tell you something."

Dave entered the sick room. At first, he

thought Steve may have already died. His skin was as white as the sheets. Then he noticed the slight rising of Steve's chest as he took shallow breaths. Dave walked quietly over to the bed and looked down, "Mr. Hunt, it's Sheriff Byrne. Did you want to see me?" There was no indication Steve had heard the sheriff. Dave leaned closer to Steve and spoke again, "Mr. Hunt, Steve. It's Sheriff Byrne."

Steve slowly turned his head and opened his eyes. "Thanks for coming Davy." His voice was so weak and raspy that Dave had to lean close to Steve with his face almost buried in Steve's chest. "There's something I've got to tell you. I don't want to die with it on my conscience." Dave had learned from experience that it was not uncommon for dying people to offer death-bed confessions.

"The skeleton you found in the attic,
I put there. It's not a woman, it's a
no-good man."

"Why don't you tell me what happened."

"It's a long story. It all started in 1935.
My daughter had just turned sixteen.
Barbara, was her name. She was so pretty,
like a lovely flower. It was hard to believe
my little girl was sixteen. She looked so
young to me.

"She and a couple of her friends went to
a carnival in town. She met a rowdy there.
He filled her head with nonsense. She
snuck off several times to be with him. He
promised to marry her and take her with
him when the carnival left. Her ma and
I knew, it wasn't really going to happen."
Steve had to stop to rest before going on.

"I'm sorry, I'm just so weak."

Although the sheriff really wanted to learn what happened, he told the patient, "It's okay, you don't have to go on. Or just take your time."

"Just be patient with me, please." Dave pulled up a chair, sat down and again leaned close to Steve. Steve took a breath and went on, "Barb even went to a second-hand store and bought a used wedding dress. She pranced around the house with it on.

"Of course, when the carnival left, so did the scoundrel. Barb cried for days. Her ma tried to comfort her. So did my son Mike. He even offered to take her with him when he went out. Barb was a lot like her ma. My wife was the nervous type. Her moods changed a lot. There was no calming Barb. She just cried and carried on.

"Then one night we heard a terrible crash.

We ran downstairs and found Barb laying in the middle of the parlor floor. There was broken glass everywhere. She had on the wedding dress and had tried to hang herself from the chandelier. It wasn't strong enough to hold her. There was blood all over her from the broken glass. I could tell her neck was broke. You know, by the way she was layin'.

"Mike picked her up. He carried her to her room. Ma washed her. We changed the sheets. In the morning I called old Doc Tucker. It's not this doctor. He's Old Doc's son. We told him Barb had fallen down the basement steps. When he passed through the dining room to go up the stairs to her room, he could see the mess in the parlor. He looked at Barb and saw all the cuts on her. He knew she hadn't fallen down any stairs. But that's what he wrote on her death certificate. He was a good man."

After disclosing this, Steve had to stop and rest. Dave sat by the bedside and waited. Eventually, Steve's voice was more resonant, and he went on with his confession, "After that my Laura just pined away. I couldn't get her to eat. She sat most of the time in her rocker, the one she had rocked Barb in as a baby. One morning I came into the living room, and there she sat in the rocker, dead. She had an inward grief that ate at her. That good-for-nothing cur pushed my wife into an early grave.

"A couple of months after Laura died, Mike and I moved into town. I just couldn't live in the farm house anymore remembering all the sorrow." Steve's breathing became more rapid and uneven.

"Steve, I think you'd better rest a bit. This is wearing you out."

"No, I want to go on. I don't want to die,

without you knowing and this- on my conscience. The next summer the carnival came back. Mike came in one day and told me he had seen the man in town. He was bragging about Barb and wanting to find her.

"That night I went to the carnival. I pretended to be friendly with that rat. I offered to buy him a drink when he got off work. I took him to a couple of bars. I got him talking about himself. His name was Wes Cook. He was from somewhere in Pennsylvania and had lived with his mother and grandmother. He didn't know his father." Steve had to stop.

The sheriff offered him a drink of water. Steve only took a tiny sip, licked his lips and continued. "He said his ma died when he was twelve. He stayed on with his grandmother until he was fifteen, then took off. He'd worked for a number of carnivals over the next ten years.

"I figured no one was going to miss him. I got him talking about Barb. Some of the things he told me made me want to kill him right then. Nonetheless, I bided my time. I told him I knew where Barb lived."

"The man didn't know who you were? Or that Barb was dead? Is that right?"

"No, I used a fake name. When he was good and drunk, I took him to the farm. I told you Mike and I had moved into town after Laura died and the farm house was empty. I showed him a bedroom window that I had opened earlier in the day. I said it was Barb's room. There was a tree near the window. I told him to climb it and get into her room and surprise her. As he was climbing the tree, I hurried around to the kitchen door and up to the bedroom. I was waiting with my gun when he came in."

Steve seemed to gain more strength as he was telling his story. "I told him who I was and what had happened to Barb. I showed him the rope Barb had used to hang herself. I made him wrap it around his neck. Then I made him put on the wedding dress. He got mad and started to take it off. So, I shot him in the leg. It started to bleed horribly. I could see the blood pulsing out of his body. I found some rags and tried to stop it. I didn't really intend for him to die. I just wanted to scare him. I couldn't get the bleeding to stop. He got weaker, and weaker, and finally just died." Exhausted, Steve sank back into his bed breathing heavily.

"Mr. Hunt, I don't need to hear the rest. Let me call the nurse to help you." Sheriff

Byrne sure didn't want to be the cause of Steve's dying while alone with him.

"I'm okay. I'm almost done. Then I can rest all I want. I'd been drinking a lot that night right along with Cook. I slumped against the wall and fell asleep. A truck on the road woke me up the next morning. The county was doing some work in the ditch in front of the house. Cook lay on the floor, cold and stiff. I didn't know what to do with him. The night seemed like a nightmare. I decided to return the next night and bury the body. But I didn't.

"Mike asked where I'd been all night. I didn't want him to get suspicious. Also, Mike and I were still farming the land around the house. We'd been baling hay. I was afraid he or someone else might see me carrying the body out of the house. So about three nights later, while Mike was out on a date with some girl, I returned to the house. I thought about burning the house down with Cook in it. I should have. I don't know why I didn't. Instead, I got a ladder and tied a rope around Cook. I got into the attic and hauled him up along with a bag filled with the bloody rags and then the rug he had been on when he died. It was soaked with blood. Fortunately, the blood hadn't gone through to the floor. After that I nailed both attic doors shut. I hoped I'd never hear about it again."

"I appreciate you telling me this Steve."

Steve Hunt looked at Sheriff Dave with tears flowing down his cheeks. "Thank you, Dave, thank you for coming and listening. Now I can rest." He closed his eyes with a look of peace.

At the behest of Sheriff Byrne, Rev. Wilcox went to visit Steve. They had a serious talk. Four days later he died with his family surrounding him.

Chapter 25

Two weeks later, Sheriff Dave Byrne sat
at his desk with Steven Hunt's file in front
of him. He had been mulling over how
to proceed. It was almost five o'clock,
quitting time. He was tired and his wife
was fixing his favorite supper, roast beef
and baked potatoes. He closed the file
and put it in the top drawer of his desk.
He got up to put on his coat and hat and
reached to turn off the light, when the
telephone rang. His first thought was to let
the night deputy answer. He decided, he
would only get home, and have to return
if the call was an emergency. He reached

over to the phone and lifted the receiver, "Sheriff Byrne."

"Thornton here, my daughter and I need to talk to you. Is now too late?"

"I'll be here, come on over." Dave called his wife and told her to keep the roast warm. He could never remember having anything except well-done meat. Half an hour later the entrance bell rang. Dave went to admit Richard Thornton and his daughter. "Come in."

"Sheriff, you know my daughter, Jeanne Riordan. Ah…we…ah…I mean…er, she has something to say." Dave was surprised at Thornton's hesitation. He was a politically influential man in the county and one of the wealthiest.

Jeanne was a petite, slender woman with short graying hair and pale brown eyes.

Dave knew of her. They were about the same age, forty-five. In her younger days she had been very pretty.

"Please sit down, both of you. How can I be of service to you?"

"Sheriff Byrne, I'm the person who broke into the Hunt home." After saying this, Jeanne began to cry. Dave looked from her to Richard with astonishment. He always kept a box of tissue on the bookcase behind him. He reached for it and handed it to Jeanne.

"Why did you do a thing like that?"

Jeanne composed herself, then continued, "My son is a senior at George Custer County High school. He is hoping to be appointed to the United States Military Academy at West Point in New York. I was afraid a scandal about my Uncle Joel

Thornton, being a draft dodger, might hurt my son's chances." Her tears started again. Her father put his arm around her and she cried into his shoulder.

Dave could barely believe what she was saying, "You're telling me, you thought what your uncle did fifty years ago would affect his great-nephew today?"

Jeanne hung her head and nodded. "I didn't mean to hurt anyone. I just wanted to see what information they had found. I'd been watching the Hunt house for days. They never go anywhere at night. Finally, they did. I got into the house; it wasn't locked. I barely got to look at the papers on their desk when I heard them return."

Sorrowfully she looked up. "I panicked and just wanted to get out. I accidentally knocked Mrs. Hunt over. I felt so terrible when that happened. Was she badly hurt?"

"No bones were broken. She had a cut on her forehead and a number of aches and bruises. But you could have killed her."

"Please, Dave, is it really necessary to scare my daughter like that? We'll pay for any damages." Mr. Thornton had regained his composure and voiced his displeasure to the sheriff's words.

"First remember, I didn't call this meeting. You were the ones who called me and asked to come here."

Sobbing into the tissue Jeanne asked, "Are you going to arrest me? Am I going to jail?"

Dave turned to Jeanne managing to ignore Richard. "Mrs. Riordan, you could be charged. What you did was very serious. Have you told anyone else about this?"

"No, well, my mother and of course my husband both know. But, no one else!"

"Go home and don't say anything to anyone. Tomorrow I'll talk to the Hunts and see how they want to proceed."

Once the two visitors left, Dave headed home. Maybe the roast wouldn't be too dried out.

Dave arrived at the Hunt house at nine the next morning. Walter was raking leaves. "Hi Davy, want to help rake?"

Dave smiled, "No Walt, I don't even have time to get my own leaves raked. I need to talk to you and Mrs. Hunt."

"Come on in. It's about time for a coffee break. You know, we haven't done anymore detecting."

Joan greeted Dave and poured three cups of coffee. Dave explained about Jeanne Riordan's confession. He asked them if they wanted to press charges.

Indignantly Walt asked, "Well, why shouldn't we?"

"Walt, stop, think for a minute. The poor lady must be so distraught. I wasn't really hurt. It wasn't as though she was here to steal."

"That woman could have caused your death! I'll never forget watching you roll down the hill into the pond."

Joan laughed, "I bet I was a sight. Walt, I don't want to charge Mrs. Riordan. We'd probably have to hire a lawyer and go to court. People would find out. I just don't care to go through all that."

Dave interrupted this banter, "There is something else I must tell you; it's about your brother." He related to them Steve's confession and finding the gun under the pine tree.

Walt sat shocked, "No wonder my brother was such a nasty, unpleasant man."

Joan added, "The poor, poor soul! Carrying around guilt all this time!"

"Now I understand why Steve wanted that house destroyed."

"Come again?" Dave looked at Walt like he had missed part of a conversation.

"My brother willed the farm and the acreage that's left to Lou and Judy. Our other three children are each getting two-thousand dollars. The rest of his money, which is a lot, is going to Lou and Judy to build a new house on the property. In Steve's will he specified the original house must be burned down. I couldn't understand why Steve wouldn't let Lou and Judy decide what they'd want to do with the place. Now I do."

Joan looked sorrowfully at her husband before asking Dave, "Does anyone else know about Steve's guilt besides Lou? I suppose if we pursue with charges against Mrs. Riordan, everyone will find out about Steve being a murderer."

"Not from me they won't. To my knowledge, no one else knows right now. The skeleton is old news and the public has a short memory. Besides, deciding about Mrs. Riordan, you must decide what you're going to tell the Gullingtons and the Seymours. And you will have to talk to Lou and Judy about how much to tell their kids."

Joan looked at Walt, "Honey, please, let the break-in rest. There's no need to cause more grief. We'll have enough with explaining about Steve."

"All right, if you say so," conceded Walt.

Joan patted Walt's hand and looked at Dave, "Do you know young Louis has been exploring everything he can find about forensic science?"

"Is that so Mrs. Hunt?"

"Yes, he's read about every article on the subject in the encyclopedias at school. Judy even drove him to the county library to check out some books. He says he wants to be a forensic archaeologist. I'm not sure what that is. Anyway, he and the other children will have to be told something."

"I think we should tell the whole truth, get it out in the open, except for who broke in, of course. It's going to get around anyway. If we're not up front about it, a lot of half-truths will circulate. Dave, there's one other thing."

"What's that Walt?"

"What about the man's remains? What happens to them? I would like to see he gets a decent burial."

"That's very kind of you. The state medical office still has them. I believe I can get them released to you for burial."

Walt and Joan decided to tell the Gullingtons and the Seymours the entire truth about Steve Hunt and his part in the killing of Wes Cook. After talking to Lou and Judy, a condensed version of the murder was decided upon.

Two evenings later, Lou gathered his four oldest children in the kitchen. "Your grandparents have something to tell you about the skeleton that was in our attic. "Betty, I want you to drive over to Grandma and Grandpa's house". He held up his hands before they could begin asking questions. "They'll tell you everything once you get there. It's chilly out tonight so put on sweaters or jackets".

The children started to leave the kitchen to get their outerwear. Lou put a hand on Betty's arm to stop her. "Betty, it's the first time you've taken the car out at night. Pay close attention to what you're doing. Don't let the others distract you."

The children arrived safely at the older Hunt's home. Immediately they began asking questions. Just like his son, Walt held up his arms. "Let's go into the kitchen. Grandma has baked a chocolate cake." Joan had said to Walt earlier, the children would be quieter and listen better if they were busy eating.

Walt sat down at the head of the table with his hands around a cup of coffee.

He was finding it difficult to talk. Finally, he explained, "In 1936, two men were out drinking and got into your house which was empty at the time. They continued their drinking. One of the men put on an old wedding dress he found hanging in a closet and danced around. The other man put a rope around the dressed-up man as a joke. Some type of argument started between the two men.

"The man dressed in the wedding gown was accidentally shot in the leg by the other man. He didn't mean to kill him. However, the bullet hit an artery and they couldn't get the bleeding to stop." Walt paused and pointed to an area on his leg. "That's why there were so many bloody rags found with the skeleton.

"The man who did the shooting was scared. He was afraid of going to prison.

He didn't want the dead man to be found. He dragged the dead man to the attic and nailed the access doors shut, hoping no one would ever find out. The guilty man is dead now. The sheriff has closed the case since there is no one to prosecute."

Darlene looked suspiciously at her grandfather, "How did the sheriff find all this out if the two men are dead?"

Joan came to her husband's rescue, "The sheriff has many resources at his disposal that the public is not aware of. Through the sheriff's investigations, he found out what happened. Maybe the guilty man told someone what he had done, before he died."

"Didn't the dead man's family miss him?" asked Betty.

"He was a drifter from out of town," replied Walt.

"Is this a secret?" asked Louis.

Walt answered his grandson, "It's not really a secret. But then again, there is really no reason to tell others. Sometimes people are curious and they might start driving to your house just to see where a murder occurred. It would be troublesome for your family to have strangers around all the time."

"Can I tell the kids at school about it?" asked Connie.

"Connie, it isn't necessary to tell everything you know," expressed Betty.

"Thank you, Betty. Connie, she's right. I would like us just to keep this information in our family."

"Okay, Grampa. Most of the kids at school have forgotten about it anyway."

Chapter 26

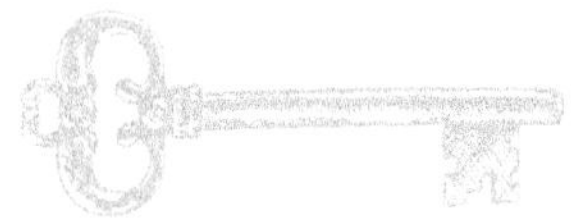

Late in the fall, the Hunt family sat around the kitchen table as night was descending over the half-harvested fields. Lou noticed his son was not eating his supper, only pretending to as he moved noodles around his plate. "Louis, what's the matter? Are you okay?"

Louis looked up from staring at his plate and saw six pairs of eyes staring back. Gloria looked at him with a noodle hanging from her lips before pulling it into her mouth and forking another. Connie's eyes were big and round as if she knew what was troubling Louis. Darlene's face was in a smirk as if saying, "For once someone else is in trouble instead of me". Betty's and Judy's faces looked almost exactly alike, motherly.

Lou looked with concern at Louis. "What's the matter Son?"

"I had some trouble in school today."

"Can you tell us? Or would you rather talk about it in private, after supper, 'man-to-man'?" Connie groaned and went back to eating. Darlene gave a sigh and sat back in her chair. Judy and Betty put down their forks and continued to look at Louis.

Louis didn't want to have another "man-to-man" talk right now. And he surely didn't want any more coffee. He put down his fork and slowly lifted his head to look at his dad. "In geography class today, Mrs.

Collins was telling us about how mountains were made. She asked if anyone had any questions. Honest! I didn't know she meant only about the mountains. I asked what was for lunch, because Mom said I could buy my lunch today and I didn't know what they were having."

"A bunch of the kids laughed. Mrs. Collins said to not be smart-alecky, and to go stand in the corner. While I was standing there, Jimmy Redman shot a spit wad at me. I made a face at him. Mary Fields saw it and laughed. Mrs. Collins thought I was trying to be funny and told me to go stand in the hall.

"While I was out in the hall, Mr. Silvers, the principal, came by and asked me why I was in the hall. I lied and told him that I had missed a test, and that I had to stand in the hall while Mrs. Collins went over it." Having finished his account, Louis lowered his head again almost to his plate.

Judy touched her son's hand and said, "You know what you have to do, don't you?"

Very quietly Louis answered, "Yes, I have to tell Mr. Silvers that I lied to him and I'm sorry." Louis lifted his head and in an insolent voice explained, "It was Mrs. Collins' fault, not mine! At least Jimmy came to me after class and said he was sorry for getting me in trouble. He's an alright guy."

Lou added, "Louis, everyone makes mistakes. Mrs. Collins probably spent several hours preparing for the geography lesson. She was disappointed and surprised at your question. That doesn't change the fact it was wrong of you to lie to Mr. Silvers."

"Yes sir. I'll go talk to him tomorrow."

"Good. How about tonight we have a game of checkers before 'Batman' comes on?"

Louis jumped up, "I'll get the checker board!"

Judy called her son back to the table, "Louis, first finish your supper."

The next morning Louis went to see the principal. Telling Mr. Silvers, the truth about being in the hall, lifted a heavy weight from Louis. He then decided to have a talk with Mrs. Collins. He hurried to her room hoping no other students would be there yet. He was in luck. Mrs. Collins stood at the blackboard writing an assignment.

He told her he was sorry for upsetting the class. He explained he really didn't understand that she only wanted questions about the mountains. He wasn't trying to be a smart-aleck. However, he didn't mention about Jimmy's spit wad.

Mrs. Collins put the chalk in the chalk tray and stood looking at him bewildered. At length, she found her voice and smiling at him said, "For you to come and talk to me is very brave and kind of you Louis. Thank you for coming. Yesterday is done and gone. Today is a new day. Let's enjoy it. I'll see you third hour."

Chapter 27

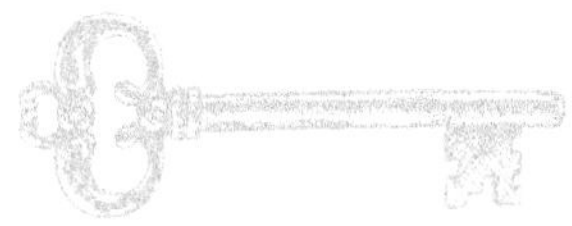

Len Rheimes watched three boys playing cowboys and Indians from his hiding place high in an oak tree in the woods. He thought, "It must be Saturday or the boys would be in school." He had been on the run for six months and discovered people seldom looked up into the trees when hunting for someone.

He could see the boys had brought their lunches with them. Could he slip in and steal them? Of course, they would know the lunches were missing, but maybe think an animal had taken them.

Very carefully and quietly he climbed down from the tree. He had gotten quite good at this. He successfully reached the lunches and had only picked one of them up when he stepped on a limb. It made a loud crack as it broke.

One boy turned, "Hey! There's a man stealing our lunches!" Len took off at a fast clip as the boys stood frozen. He knew they would beat it home to tell their parents. At least one parent would realize it was the man the police were looking for and contact the authorities. Now it was more urgent than ever, he had to find a hiding place.

Hurrying to the other side of the small woods he looked across a harvested field and spied a cement block milk house. When it was totally dark, he crept to the building, which was not locked. "The fools!

Don't nobody lock buildings around here?"
He was sure the milk house was no longer
used for its original purpose. It appeared
now to be used for storage. Scattered
around the room were several rusting milk
cans, an old mattress, some broken chairs,
and what looked like badminton equipment
and a croquet set. He looked closer at
the chairs to see if they were usable.
One looked like it might hold him. He sat
down and finally investigated the lunch.
"A peanut butter and jelly sandwich. Don't
kids eat anything else?" Wrapped in wax
paper were three homemade chocolate
chip cookies. He inhaled the sandwich
then slowly ate the cookies.

"I got to have something to drink. I didn't
see a pump. Maybe I missed it. As soon as
the lights in the house are out, I'll go look
for one. What I wouldn't give for a cup of
coffee! Maybe I should turn myself in."

Len discarded the idea. He knew enough about the law to realize if anyone was dead, which he was pretty sure there was, he could be charged with murder, even if he hadn't pulled the trigger.

"Say, if today is Saturday that means tomorrow is Sunday. Maybe I can get into the house when the people go to church." He laid down on the mattress to rest. It was dirty and smelled, then again it was the softest thing he had slept on in months.

About two o'clock in the morning, Len opened the door and walked around. He didn't see a pump. "Maybe I should take a chance and go inside." He had never entered an occupied house. He cautiously stepped on the first porch step, then the next. With care he reached the door and tried the handle; it opened. "What idiots to leave the doors unlocked!" He entered the kitchen and looked around. Sitting on a small table was a glass! In it he could see some liquid. He took a drink; it was water. The small amount quieted his raging thirst.

He went to the sink and filled the glass, drinking the precious water and filled the glass again, this time drinking it more slowly. Next, he checked the refrigerator. There was a plate of left-over fried chicken. He took two pieces and skillfully distributed the remaining three pieces around the plate hoping no one would notice any missing. Wrapping the chicken in a towel hanging on the refrigerator door handle, he stuffed it into his pocket.

Several home-canned jars of fruit and vegetables sat on a shelf, gleaming in the moon light. He lifted a jar of peaches and a jar of tomato juice. He then repositioned the remaining jars to fill where the two jars had been sitting.

As he was about to leave, he spied an overcoat hanging on a hook by the door. "Maybe the coat won't be missed right away. Then I'll be gone." He took the risk of taking the coat and silently left the house returning to the milk house. After eating the chicken and drinking a portion of the juice, he put the coat on, laid down on the smelly mattress and fell asleep.

The noise of a motor running woke him. He peeked out the door. The man was going to mow the lawn. "These people must not go to church!" Soon three children came out to play. He watched them as he ate the peaches using his knife as a fork. Most of his day was spent sleeping. There was too much activity around the yard for him to leave the milk house. Late in the afternoon, the family piled into the car and left.

Len waited several minutes before reentering the house. "Maybe I can find some money to pay for a bus ticket and get out of the area." He looked through various drawers in the kitchen and dining room. He only found a bit of change. He went upstairs to search the bedrooms. The first room was a child's bedroom. He saw a piggy bank sitting on a dresser. Less than a dollar in coins fell out when he broke it open. He moved on to the next room which was the parents' room.

 Immediately his eyes fell on a wallet resting on a chest-of-drawers. Then he heard a door open and footsteps running across the floor and up the stairs. In a panic, Len wormed his way under the bed just as a boy came into the room. Len could only see the boy's feet as he walked around the room.

The boy stuck his head out a window, "Hey Dad, are you sure your wallet was on your dresser? I can't find it anywhere." His dad yelled something unrecognizable. "Okay, I'll look in the kitchen." The boy left the bedroom and ran down the stairs.

Covered in dust bunnies, Len crawled out from under the bed. "Boy, what a lousy housekeeper." Len wasn't sure what to do. He figured the man would be coming up to look for the wallet himself. Nervously Len crept down the stairs. He could hear the boy banging about in the kitchen, then the kitchen door opened. A window in the living room was open. Len rushed across the floor and hurdled himself out. He ran as fast as he could across the new mown grass and into an unharvested corn field.

It was easy to get lost in the over six-foot-high stalks. The leaves had turned brown and the ears were bent down ready for harvesting. Len continued walking through the stalks.

He came out of the corn field and entered the woods. Continuing to walk, he heard someone coming. He did his usual trick and climbed a tree. Several dried leaves fell as he went up as far as he dared. It wouldn't be much longer and he wouldn't be able to hide in trees. He was tired and scared. Two men passed beneath him and never looked up. Len waited until it was dark and slowly climbed down. "Whatever am I going to do? I should have stayed in the Army."

He turned back toward the corn field and pulled a cob of corn off one stalk, removed the husks and ate some of the hard kernels. About an hour later he experienced terrible stomach cramps. Laying between two rows of unharvested corn he rolled into a fetal position and found himself sobbing.

Monday, Len was having difficulty breathing; every time he took a breath his chest hurt. Weak and walking between the woods and corn field, he saw a white clapboard house some distance away. A large equipment shed was near the back of the property. As the sun was setting, he cautiously walked to the shed and opened the door. It was so full of farm implements, tools, bicycles, and other play items, there was barely any place for him to sit. Len figured it must be about five o'clock. Just as he was drifting into a troubled sleep, he heard what he thought was a gunshot.

Minutes later he was alerted to steps

approaching the shed. He picked up a hoe and waited. The door opened, he blindly swung the hoe and ran. That night sleeping in the open he started coughing. Cold and hungry, besides having a dreadful thirst, he was utterly miserable.

Chapter 28

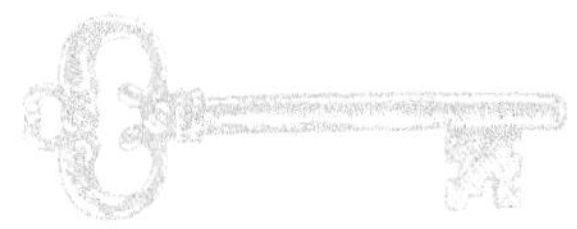

The next day the Hunt children got off the school bus. Louis sprinted down the drive and came bounding into the house. "Ma, you'll never guess what I heard at school today."

Judy was in the kitchen making noodles for supper. "Good afternoon, Louis. What did you hear at school today? Something good I hope."

"Sorry, hi Mom. Yesterday, Norman Echols's dad shot a skunk and told Norm's older brother Wayne to bury it. Wayne went to their shed to get a shovel and a man was in there. The man hit him with a hoe. He had to go to the hospital to get a hundred stitches."

By this time Betty, Darlene and Connie had come into the kitchen. Betty laughed, "It wasn't a hundred stitches. Wayne was in school today. He's in my first hour Geometry class. Everyone was asking what happened. So, Miss White had him tell the class what happened. He said a man was hiding in their shed. When Wayne opened the door, the man tried to hit him with a hoe and missed. The man dropped the hoe and ran. Wayne fell on the hoe and cut his arm. His dad drove him to the hospital and he said he has six stitches. All there was to see was just a large bandage on his arm."

Connie entered the conversation, "Well, my friend Bonnie said there was a man in their house Sunday. Her dad was taking them to get ice cream and forgot his wallet. They came back home and Bonnie's brother went in to get the wallet. He couldn't find it so her dad came in and a man was there. He jumped through a window and ran into the corn field next to their house. Bonnie said her dad chased the man until he lost him in the corn field.

"The sheriff came and took fingerprints. He told them the man probably wouldn't come back but to keep their doors locked. Bonnie was mad because the man must have taken her dad's wallet so they didn't have any money to get the ice cream."

Darlene frowned and looked at her mother, "It must be the same man. Do you think it's the man who got away in the beer garden robbery last spring?"

"Yes, it probably is. The sheriff has been on WTAC radio several times today and cautioned people to lock their doors and to report any strangers they may see."

"Mommy, do our doors lock?" Connie walked to the back-kitchen door and looked at it very closely.

"That's a good question Sugar. I'm sure they did at one time." She could tell the children were frightened. "Let's play a game. Everyone look for keys, find all you can. We'll try them in the doors. The one who finds a key that fits a door will get ten cents." Louis dumped his books and lunch box on the kitchen table, barely missing the homemade egg noodles drying there. Connie and Louis started looking in drawers, on shelves and in closets. Betty and Darlene stood in the kitchen undecided what to do. "If you girls don't want to help look for keys, there are towels in the dryer that need folding."

"Mother! Have you been carrying baskets of laundry up and down the basement stairs? You know the doctor told you not to lift and to only climb stairs when it was absolutely necessary." Betty had her hands on her hips and looked at her mother with a scowl on her face. "Don't you think I'm capable of keeping the laundry done! Aren't I doing an adequate job?"

Judy was very touched at Betty's concern. There had been some problems with this pregnancy. Twice the doctor ordered bed rest for Judy because of spotting. The second time it happened, he told her to limit climbing stairs and absolutely no lifting. She was pleased how the children had stepped up to help. Betty was keeping the laundry done. Darlene saw that the carpets were kept vacuumed and mopped the linoleum floors. Connie did her best at sweeping the kitchen floor. Little

Gloria tried to dust and Lou and Louis did the dishes.

"I'm sorry Sweetheart. I really didn't lift or carry anything. Gloria got chocolate all over her favorite top. She was upset that it was going to be ruined. I washed it out in cold water and then decided to launder it. I tossed the blouse in with some towels and clothes that were already in the basement. You and all of my family are doing such a good job helping me! I have no complaints about the excellent job you're doing with the laundry."

"Well, from now on, just let whatever needs immediate washing sit in cold water and I'll take care of it as soon as I get home."

"Yes dear."

Several keys were found. Louis and Connie went around to the doors trying them in the locks. Connie had a key that locked the kitchen back door. Louis's key fit the living room, dining room and the second door in the kitchen leading to the side porch. Louis said he should get thirty cents. Connie argued it was only one key so he should only get ten cents. Judy suggested twenty-five cents to which Louis agreed.

"What about the door in my bedroom?" asked the worried Louis.

Judy assured him, "We do have a key to that door. It was in the upper left-hand drawer of the buffet. Let me see the other keys you two found." She looked over each key, "I'm pretty sure this is the one that fits."

"That's one of the keys I found! I get another dime," yelled Connie.

Judy gave Connie an exasperated look,

"We're not deaf, Connie. Please don't talk so loudly. Louis, go to your room and try the key."

Louis raced up to his room and was back down in only a couple of minutes. "It fits! I locked the door. What should I do with the key?"

"Put it by your door so we know where the key is, in case we need to go out that way."

"Can the door in Betty's room be opened?"

"No Connie, there is the big wardrobe in front of it and I remember locking the door when we moved in. There is no sidewalk that goes to it so no one would even think a door is there."

Lou arrived home from work that evening, and sat quietly listening as his children recounted all that had happened. He didn't tell them he had already heard about the events of the day.

After the children were in bed Lou checked each outside door. He walked past Betty's bedroom door and saw it was open. He peeked in to say good-night. Her bed was empty.

Lou went upstairs and stopped at Darlene's door. He could hear his two daughters talking. He gently knocked on the door. "Yes," came a voice from inside the room.

"It's your old man. Can I come in?"

"Sure Daddy."

Lou peeked his head into the room. The light was out and Darlene and Betty were snuggled up to each other. "I was just downstairs and saw you weren't in your room Betty. Are you okay?"

"I didn't like sleeping downstairs by myself. It's a little scary."

"That's okay Sweetheart. I understand. This will be over soon. The man can't hold out much longer. Go to sleep now and God will be awake all night looking after us."

Chapter 29

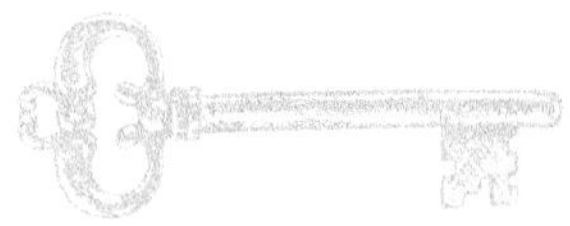

October sixth couldn't have been a more perfect Indian Summer day. A southern breeze helped to keep the temperature warm. A few puffy clouds occasionally blocked out the sun for a few seconds. Sean had the day off. He and Mavis were going on a picnic. Mavis had not scheduled any appointments for the day. A couple of her regular Wednesday customers were upset. She didn't care. She felt today was going to be a very special day. She was wearing her best pink sweater and matching pink box pleated skirt. She had worked over an hour fixing her hair and make-up.

They went to a scenic picnic area beside the gravel pit. The pit was surrounded by trees of all colors; red, and gold, orange and brown, with a few green pine trees as accents. The pit was no longer worked. Someone had added sand to one side to make a beach. In summer, the place would have been packed with swimmers.

Today, no one else was there. Neither one said anything; both were glad they were alone together. Mavis spread a blanket on the ground while Sean got out the picnic basket. "Mavis, before we eat there is something I want to ask you."

"Yes Sean?" Suddenly the wind changed and huge black clouds appeared over the horizon and the heavens opened. Torrents of rain descended. The wind scattered the picnic items in all directions. Some landed in the wind-stirred water of the gravel pit. Both laughed as they gathered what they could and dashed to the car.

They were drenched. It didn't matter to either of them. With no hesitation, Sean drew Mavis to him, "I really like you, Mavis. As a matter-of-fact, I love you! When I look into your beautiful green eyes and touch your soft tender skin, I can't imagine living my life without you. All I want is for us to spend the rest of our lives together. I know with the kind of job I have it won't be easy for you. If you can put up with that and me, you would make me the happiest man in the world by marrying me."

He then reached into his breast pocket and took out a box. Opening it he continued, "This diamond isn't real big and the jeweler said if you don't like the design, we can exchange it. Would you do me the honor of becoming my wife?"

Mavis looked at the ring and started to cry. "Oh Sean, it's beautiful. I'd marry you even if there was no ring. I love you more than you could ever know."

Sean slipped the ring on Mavis's finger. It was a little too big. He took her in his arms and kissed her passionately.

The rain did not let up. They sat quietly in each other's arms watching it come down. "What kind of a wedding do you want? I hope you don't want to wait a long time because I'd like to marry you today," whispered Sean.

"This may sound silly to you, but I'd like to get married at a Sunday evening church service. The people who come to church that night would be the ones who get to see us get married. It would be a kind of a gift for coming to church. And I want to be married in a blue brocade suit, wearing blue velvet shoes and carrying blue roses!"

Sean took Mavis's chin in one of his hands and lifted her head, "Anything is all right with me as long as it's soon." He bent lovingly to her and kissed her tenderly. Then he straightened and smiled, "Right now I'm really getting hungry." They didn't dare go to either house for lunch. They were aware too many people in town kept a constant vigil on their every move. Sean started the car, "Let's go to **Aunt Patti's Kitchen** for lunch and get married this Sunday!"

Chapter 30

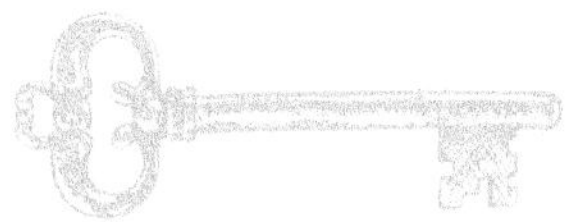

Judy put Gloria down for her nap, then sorted through stored baby clothes. Looking at the little garments, a smile crossed her lips as she rubbed her belly. "A few more weeks little one and you'll be here."

The rain had changed to a cold drizzle. Len walked towards the house from the backyard. "That's Judy's house. She's always been good to me. At school, when she saw the other kids being mean to me, she made them stop. Maybe she'll give me something to eat."

Judy heard the kitchen door open. "Now who can that be? Oh, I forgot to lock the kitchen door after the kids left for school. Maybe it's Walt and Joan." It was not unusual for them to occasionally visit unexpectedly. But she hadn't heard a car.

Judy put the clothes away and headed down the stairs. She stopped abruptly at the doorway between the dining room and kitchen. Staring at her was a barely recognizable Leonard Rheimes. His drawn face was the color of dirty chalk. His rheumy eyes were sunken and red-crusted. He was five or six years younger than Judy but now looked much older. His older sister, Leah, and Judy were friends. Len was considered a "black sheep" of an otherwise good family. Judy remembered him as always being in trouble at school, and with the police.

Len walked to the table and collapsed into a chair. "Judy, I'm starving, give me somethin' to eat. I'm not going to hurt you. Please, help me." He said this through cracked lips. He coughed a hacking deep cough. His clothes were filthy and ragged. His beard and shaggy hair were matted. Judy guessed he had lost fifteen or twenty pounds from his already modest frame. In his hand was a gun.

Judy willed herself to stay calm, as she went to the refrigerator, and removed milk, butter and lunch meat. "You must have been living awfully rough these past couple of months." She set the items on the table and headed for the bread box. Len grabbed the meat and began devouring it. Judy buttered two slices of bread and poured a glass of milk. Len laid the gun on the table and picked up the glass with trembling hands. The glass was instantly emptied. He started to cough and hold his chest.

He looked at Judy through dull, pale eyes. "Hand me the bread." Judy unobtrusively placed a kitchen towel over the gun as she handed Len the bread. After eating the bread and drinking another glass of milk, Len appeared to sink. "I'm so tired. All I want to do is sleep. I've been hiding in the woods for months." He continued to cough as he related this information to Judy.

"Do you mean the woods next to our field?" Len nodded. A chill ran through Judy. Louis and his friends had played in those woods all summer. Judy pushed down the fear and panic that threatened to overwhelm her.

She pointed to the pantry, "Len, there is a bed of blankets on the floor in the pantry. My daughter sometimes naps there when

I'm working here in the kitchen. Go lay down for a few minutes. I have some cough medicine. One of my children was sick last winter and the doctor prescribed it for her cough." She moved to a cupboard as she was talking. She showed Len the label. "See, it says 'Take one teaspoon every four hours for cough'. I'll give you two teaspoons, you'll feel better."

Len sat gazing into space while rambling on. "I can't. I have to hide. You'll call the sheriff. Oh, I just want to sleep." He started coughing violently again.

"I won't call the sheriff," Judy opened the bottle and poured the medicine into a tablespoon. Len looked at her then took the medicine. She offered him a second tablespoon which he swallowed. Getting up, he walked to the pantry and collapsed onto the little bed.

Judy stood silently until Len began to snore. She picked up the gun and as quickly as she could, went upstairs. Removing the lid of the toilet tank she dropped the gun in, replaced the lid and set some toys on the lid. She went to Gloria's room and gathered her up in a quilt. Gloria woke up, "Mommy, what are you doing? Why are you wrapping me in this blanket?"

"Shush, Baby. This is a game. You must stay quiet."

"I'm still tired. I don't want to play. Can't I go back to bed?"

"No. Just stay quiet."

Judy was so thankful for the outside stairway off Louis's bedroom which he had spoken about last night. Judy unlocked the door with the key Louis had placed on his dresser next to the door. "Thank you, Lord, for giving Lou the wisdom to put in this door." As quietly as possible, carrying a very unhappy Gloria, she used the stairway to leave the house and struck out into the rain. Gloria continued to be obstinate and ask questions. Fortunately, the stairs were on the opposite side of the house from the kitchen. She carried Gloria across the lawn to the front of the property. A post and wire fence enclosed the yard. She lifted Gloria, still in the quilt and forlornly complaining, over the fence. Gloria landed on her stomach and face and began to cry. Judy ignored her. She still had to figure out how she was going to get across in her condition. Then she felt the first contraction. "No! God, please. It's still four weeks before the baby is due. Not now, please!"

There was no time to lose. Len might wake up at any moment and start looking for her. Judy considered telling Gloria to run to the neighbors, a good half-mile away. She knew Gloria wouldn't do that. She was now sitting on the quilt crying. Judy put her right hand on the top of the nearest post and started climbing on the wire. Reaching the top, she swung her left leg over and started down the other side. "Thank you, Lord, thank you."

"Come on Gloria, we have to walk to Mrs. Reed's house."

"I can't, I'm only in my socks, I don't have on any shoes. Mommy, I don't like this game. I want to go back to our house."

Judy only looked at Gloria and sighed. Then she realized the ditch separated them from the road. "Gloria, you have to jump the ditch."

"I can't." Gloria stood, put her hands on her

hips, tightened her lips, and narrowed her eyes at Judy.

Judy picked up Gloria and tried to toss her over the ditch. Gloria grabbed hold of Judy and both landed in the muddy cold water. Gloria sat in the middle of the ditch crying. Judy strengthening her resolve, grabbed Gloria and hauled both of them up to the gravel road. Another contraction gripped her. When it had passed, she took Gloria's hand and headed for the Reeds, a half mile away. "Mommy, I can't walk. I don't have any shoes on. I'm in my stocking feet."

Judy sadly looked at Gloria and wondered what to do. "Please, God I need your help. Please do something!" No sooner had the prayer left her lips when she heard a car coming. "Oh Jesus, thank you, thank you." Judy recognized Sean at the steering wheel and Mavis beside him.

Sean stopped and jumped out. As he did so he reached into the back seat and grabbed a blanket. Wrapping it around the shaking woman he guided her into the back seat. "Mrs. Hunt, what's wrong? Why are you standing here in the rain?"

Mavis had come around from the other side of the car carrying another blanket. She wrapped it around Gloria, picked her up and carried her back to the passenger's side of the back seat. Gloria huddled close to Judy.

"Sean, Leonard Rheimes is in the house."

"What?"

"He's asleep on a pallet in the pantry just off the kitchen. He's in bad shape. When he fell asleep, I took the gun he had with him and dropped it in the toilet tank upstairs."

Judy had to quit talking when another contraction seized her.

"Mrs. Hunt what's wrong? Are you okay?"

"I'm early, but I think the baby is coming."

"Mavis, take Mrs. Hunt to the hospital and call the sheriff as soon as you can." Mavis slid behind the steering wheel.

Before Mavis had a chance to start the car, Judy put her hand on Mavis' shoulder and looked at Sean. "Sean, if you go along the south side of the house, Len won't be able to see you if he's awake. There are outside stairs. They can't be seen from the kitchen either. That's how we got out." Sean nodded and started for the house. He jumped the ditch with ease and, using one hand on a post, swung his body over the fence. Judy couldn't help envying him.

Mavis was driving as fast as she dared.

While on the way to the hospital, Judy asked Mavis to call her in-laws to pick up the children after school. "Don't tell them what's wrong. Just say the children must not go home. Make up something if you have to. Can you also call Lou's company and ask them to have him come to the hospital?" This last request was said through clenched teeth as Judy experienced another contraction.

Mavis started laying on the horn when she turned into the hospital's emergency lane. Two attendants hastened to the car as she pulled up to the ER entrance. She jumped out and opened the back door. Judy started to get out. An attendant instantly sized up the situation and got a wheelchair. Judy was whisked off. Mavis looked at Gloria who sat petrified. She reached into the back seat and lifted Gloria who clung to Mavis' neck until Mavis had to plead with her to loosen her grip. "Where is my Mommy going? I'm scared."

"It's all right Sweetie. Mama's going to have your new baby. I'll park the car. Then we can go into the hospital."

Judy had already been pushed into another part of the hospital by the time Mavis and Gloria entered the waiting room. Mavis went over to the receptionist's desk. The receptionist was a longtime customer of Tangles. "Ella, I need to use the phone to make some emergency calls."

Ella looked at Mavis and saw the urgency on her face. Without saying a word, she pushed the telephone towards her, "Push nine to get an outside line."

Mavis called the sheriff's office and told Thelma about Sean. Thelma said Sean had already called in and help was on the way.

Next, she called the senior Hunt house; Mr. Hunt answered. He was surprised to hear Mavis's voice and at first tried to make small talk. "I'm sorry Mr. Hunt. Judy has an emergency. I can't talk more right now. She asked me to tell you to pick up your grandchildren from school. It's important. Don't let any of them take the bus home. Can you do that? "

"Sure I can. What's wrong?"

"I don't have time to explain now. I'll come by in a bit and tell you everything. Please just be sure none of the kids goes home." She hung up the phone and dialed Lou's work number. A secretary answered. Mavis explained Judy was in the hospital and Lou needed to come as quickly as possible. The secretary said she would locate him and pass on the information.

Mavis hung up the receiver and pushed

back the telephone. "Thanks Ella. I appreciate your help. I'd like to give you a free haircut for letting me use the phone."

"No, that's not necessary. What about the little girl? Is she all right?"

Mavis looked down at Gloria and was startled at how she looked. Her eyes were saucers and she was shaking all over. Mavis knelt down and picked Gloria up. She sat down in a chair and held Gloria, rocking her back and forth. "Would it be possible to get Gloria some dry clothes?"

Ella got up, "Follow me." She took them into a back office. "I'll be right back." In minutes, Ella returned with pediatric pajamas, a pink robe, some slippers that looked like bunnies, a towel and a damp wash cloth.

Mavis washed Gloria and changed

her clothes. "You're going to be the cat's pajamas!"

"I don't want to be the cat's pajamas. I just want my Mommy."

"I know you do Darling." Mavis sat down in a chair and beckoned Gloria to come sit on her lap. She gave Gloria a hug and began singing softly. After only a few minutes Gloria's eyes closed in sleep. Mavis continued to quietly sing.

A knock at the door awakened Gloria. The door opened and Lou stuck his head in. "Daddy!" Gloria flew across the room into Lou's arms and started to cry. "Daddy, Mommy told me we were playing a game. But I didn't like it. And now they took Mommy away."

"It's all right Gloria. Mommy's upstairs with your new baby brother."

Mavis asked, "Are Judy and the baby okay?"

"Judy's doing just fine. She's a real trooper. The baby came four weeks early. He's kind 'a small. Doc says he'll probably have to stay in the hospital a couple of extra days. I just hope Judy gets to stay too. She sure won't like going home without her baby."

"Can we go see them, Daddy?"

"No Sugar, I'm sorry. The hospital won't let children visit. You'll have to wait until Mommy and the baby come home." Gloria started to pout.

Mavis took Gloria's hand and said, "Gloria, you're a big sister now. You're no longer the baby. Let's go see Louis and your sisters. You can be the first to tell them about the new baby and the adventure you had with Mommy this afternoon.

Gloria sighed and looked at Mavis then to her daddy. "I guess so. Daddy, are you coming over to Grandma's?"

"I'm going to see Mommy, and then I'll be there. After that you can have a ride home in my truck!"

Gloria gave a big smile and hugged Lou. She shook her finger at Lou, "Don't be too long Daddy."

Chapter 31

While Mavis was driving to the hospital, Sean retraced Judy's route. Cautiously he made his way along the house and up the stairs. Quietly opening the door to Louis's room, he removed his ankle revolver, and crossed the bedroom to the hall. Then he silently descended the house stairs, stopped and listened. Loud snoring came from the kitchen area. Walking through the dining room he saw the telephone on the wall by the dining room door. Before using it to call for backup, he entered the kitchen and saw Len still sleeping on the pallet in the pantry. "Boy, he sure does look a wreck."

Quietly, he returned to the dining room and called the office. He explained the situation, asking for backup. He decided to let Len sleep until assistance came. An electric coffee pot was on, so he poured himself a cup, sat down at the kitchen table in view of the pantry and helped himself to some cookies sitting on the table. Ten minutes later, two squad cars drove up the lane to the house. Sean met the sheriff and a new hire, Deputy Richard Corley, at the door.

Sheriff Byrne felt fortunate to have Corley, a giant of a man. He was just out of the Army where he had been in the Military Police. He and his wife were both from the area and planned to remain here. When Dave was interviewing Corley, he had asked him about his future plans. With a wicked grin Corley had answered, "Sir, I hope to be sheriff one day. That is, after you've retired."

Dave took one look at Len and told Sean to call for an ambulance. While the three waited for the ambulance they drank coffee and ate more cookies.

Dave woke up Len when the ambulance arrived. He looked up at the cluster of men, submissive and accepting, saying, "I should have stayed in the Army". Len was so weak he had to be lifted onto the stretcher by the ambulance crew. Deputy Corley handcuffed Len. Dave didn't say anything even though he thought it wasn't really necessary. "Sean, you ride in the ambulance with Len to the hospital. We'll follow you."

At the hospital Len was given oxygen and

examined by a physician who ordered an x-ray. Dave told Sean he could leave as it was his day off. Sean left the building just in time to see Mavis and Gloria walking out. The three went to the senior Hunt's home.

Deputy Corley and Dave stayed in the examination room. They watched unobtrusively as Len was poked and prodded, first by one medical person then another. The physician motioned for Dave to follow him out into the hall. "Sheriff, this is a very sick man. He needs to stay here for treatment or he will die. He is likely to die even with treatment."

"Do what you need to do. I'll arrange for a twenty-four-hour watch on him." Dave sighed and stuck his head into the partially open door. "Richard, stay here with the prisoner. Don't leave him alone for even a minute. Understood?"

"Yes sir."

Every time Corley talked to Dave he started or ended with 'Sir'. Dave had intended to tell Corley he didn't always have to call him 'Sir'. He decided this was not the time. Driving back to the office Dave knew it was extra duty for all his men. Even he would have to take a turn. No one would be getting any time off for a while.

Late in October, Rev. Wilcox conducted a grave side service for Wes Cook, the secret skeleton from the attic. Only eight people were in attendance; Walter and Joan Hunt, Henry and Beverly Gullington, Martin and Harriet Seymour and Lou and Judy Hunt. As the couples left the short service, they saw another fresh grave being dug. It was for Leonard Rheimes. He had not survived the pneumonia.

Epilogue

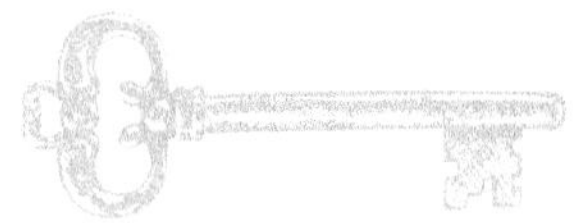

When Mavis told her mother the kind of wedding she wanted, Mrs. Hampton almost shouted, "I'll not have my only daughter getting married at a "surprise wedding" and in a blue suit. "You know what everyone will think!" Sean and his future father-in-law sat around the kitchen table drinking coffee and musing over the tête-à-tête in the living room. A compromise was finally reached between the mother and daughter. A small candle lit-wedding was held at the church the first Saturday in November. Mavis wore a mid-length white organza gown carrying blue roses. Betty in a royal blue dress was the maid-of-honor.

Thanksgiving Day dawned clear and cold. Judy had been up most of the night with a colicky baby. Little Walter Mitchel was finally asleep. He had done well, gaining weight, eating and sleeping. Judy was surprised at this latest development. After six children she shouldn't have been. She now lay in bed dozing. Lou was up early to look after the other children and to keep them quiet.

To everyone's surprise, Harriet Seymour had invited everyone to her house for dinner. This included Norman Makenzie, the retired pharmacist, and the Gullingtons who had no children and would be alone for the holiday.

Judy couldn't believe Harriet had also given the maid, Flora, a four-day weekend and a bonus so she could visit her family in Arkansas. What was the world coming to!

Dinner was scheduled for two o'clock. Joan and Bev planned to arrive early to help Harriet, each bringing a couple of dishes. Judy was glad she hadn't been asked to help. She offered to have Betty and Darlene also go early, but Harriet said no, they could help serve.

Judy rested in bed thinking about Christmas; "This coming Christmas will be the last one in this house". She was a bit melancholy, glad to be getting a new modern home yet sad about leaving the old house. There really was nothing special about this house. There was no fancy woodwork or beautiful hardwood floors. The one bathroom didn't even have a tub.

 For fifteen years she had carried dirty clothes to the basement to wash. Then in warm weather she carried the same clothes, now wet, up the stairs to hang on the line. It would be so nice to have a main floor laundry room with a modern washer and dryer.

She and Lou would now have a main floor bedroom with a master bathroom. There were going to be two more bathrooms upstairs plus a guest powder room on the main floor.

There was not one counter in the old kitchen. All Judy's cooking and baking had been prepared on the kitchen table. She was making sure the new kitchen had plenty of counter space.

Judy looked at her baby, "It's hard to believe all that has transpired in just the past few months. And to think it all started with a game of hide-and-seek on a cold and snowy, April Fool's day." There has been sadness, still much good has come out of the experiences. It really is true; God did use what happened for our good. Old secrets that should never have been kept are now known. Ill feelings between people have been acknowledged and mended and new friendships created.

"Yes, God is good."

The End

Aknowledgments

I wish my parents were still with us. I don't remember ever thanking them for growing up in a home with love and security. I think they would have liked reading this book. My sisters and brother also need to be acknowledged for contributing to a happy and sometimes challenging childhood.

John, my best friend, husband of sixty years, and steadfast editing buddy is owed much. Without his unwavering support I'm not sure I would have finished this book. He has read, and listened to this book many times. I so appreciate his helpful contributions. Sometimes I feel he should be listed as co-author.

Lynda Small is a cousin to whom I am grateful. She offered many helpful suggestions.

Each of the staff at Typewriter Creative is a jewel. They are part of a terrific team of workers doing an incredible job. I highly value their concentration to the details it takes to publish a book. Thank you, each one, for your exceptional work. It has been a blessing working with you.

About the Author

Marsha Sabin Pester began writing after retiring from a career in nursing and teaching school. Her first book, **Secret Circumstance** was published in 2022. Although **Secret Skeleton** is not an autobiography, there are some similarities.

Marsha is from Michigan and lived in an old farmhouse. She has three sisters and one brother. Her dad was a truck driver. On a few occasions she got to ride along with him on short trips. She has been married for sixty years to her best friend, John. God blessed them with a daughter, Deborah and a son, Timothy. Debbie went home to be with Jesus in 2016. Marsha and John claim eight grandchildren and one great-grandson. If you want to contact Marsha, you can at marshapester@gmail.com.